Guarding the Quarterback

Little Hondo Press
Contact: littlehondopress@yahoo.com

Guarding the Quarterback – Champions of the Heart – Book 1
Copyright © 2016 Elizabeth Matis
Digital ISBN: 978-0-9908848-4-2
Print ISBN: 978-0-9908848-5-9

Print Edition

Photo and Cover Design by: Sara Eirew Photographer
Editor: Karen Dale Harris

www.lizmatis.com
elizabethmatis@gmail.com
Sign up for my newsletter www.lizmatis.com

Also by Liz Matis

Playing For Keeps – Fantasy Football Romance – Season 1

Going For It – Fantasy Football Romance – Season 2

Huddle Up – Fantasy Football Romance – Season 3

The Quarterback Sneak – Fantasy Football Romance – Season 4

Fantasy Football Romance – Box Set: Seasons 1-4

Summer Dreaming – Hot in the Hamptons – Book 1

Love By Design

Real Men Don't Drink Appletinis

Coming soon:

Playing For Gelato – Champions of the Heart – Book 2

Guarding the Quarterback

Miss Congeniality meets The Bodyguard

Alexa Reeves

The quarterback of the NY Kings has a body to die for, and as Dean Walker's bodyguard I'm right in the line of fire. If that's not dangerous enough, I'm posing as his girlfriend to keep close. Yet, that isn't the worst part. He says I need a makeover to pass as his arm candy. Jerk. The more time I spend with him, the more my undercover role blurs with reality, and I'll lose more than my job if I step over the line and into his bed.

Dean Walker

Let's get something straight. I didn't ask for protection, especially in the form of a female. Isn't a death threat just another day in the life of a NY quarterback? Still, the owner of the team forces me to accept a security detail led by the tiny but tough Alexa Reeves.

But who is the real Alexa? The bodyguard, sworn to protect me, or the made-over vixen, determined to drive me crazy? As the stalker closes in, I realize I've put more than my life in her hands. Will Alexa safeguard my heart as fiercely as my body?

Dedication

This book is dedicated to the Janet Lane Walter's Tuesday night critique group: Janet Lane Walters, Yolanda Sly, Kelly Janicello, Tara Andrews, Gianna Simone, Elizabeth Shore, Elf Ahearn, Claire Ruane, Debbie Cracovia, and especially to the late Kat Attalla.

Acknowledgements

Thanks to author, Jami Davenport for letting my New York Kings play against her Seattle Steelheads team.

Thanks to authors, Allie Boniface and Yolanda Sly who are the unfortunate souls who muddle through my 1st drafts.

Guarding the Quarterback

Champions of the Heart – Book 1

by Liz Matis

Chapter 1

Dean Walker

I PUNCHED THE digits of the secretary's number into my contacts. Too bad the gorgeous blonde only offered up her body and not the reason why I'd been summoned.

If I could pinpoint what I'd done to deserve a trip to my boss's office, I could draw up a defense before facing the owner of the New York Kings. Could be any number of things. Sleeping with one of the coach's daughters during training camp to trash-talking to the press about our crosstown rivals, the Cougars. Or maybe it was my lackluster performance on the field during the last game.

It was kind of like being a kid again and your parents asking you what you did wrong while you debated which wrong to admit. I'd learned long ago to play dumb and not incriminate myself.

The secretary took a call, so I jammed my six-foot-four frame into a chair designed for someone who was a foot shorter. I'd stand but I knew I'd pace the waiting room like a caged beast. *Can't let them see you sweat.* I tugged at my collar, feeling out of my element away from the field where I conducted my business and in a place where billion-dollar deals were negotiated.

Checking my phone, I wondered what could possibly be keeping my agent from helping his multimillion-dollar client.

On cue, Carlos entered the room, looking every bit the shark he was. His grease-black hair slicked back in a sixties pompadour was a contrast to the short air-dry look I sported for convenience sake. He was unflappable in his pressed business suit while my khaki-clad legs bounced like a jackhammer. I pressed my hands on my thighs to stop the motion. Carlos spoke with the secretary and then slid into the seat next to me.

"What did you do now?" he asked in a tight whisper.

"Nothing out of the ordinary." But ordinary for me was some crazy shit.

Carlos shook his head. "You're a high maintenance fuck."

I laughed. "Don't bitch because I make you earn your percentage."

"A lousy three percent," complained Carlos. "Don't know why I bother with you football meatheads."

"For the ten percent you get on our endorsement deals." Thank God the league capped agent fees at three percent of a player's salary, otherwise I'd be paying ten for that too. "The trading deadline is days away. You don't think...?" I wasn't about to chance bad luck by finishing the sentence.

Carlos threw me an annoyed look. "Your contract is iron clad. Besides Billings wouldn't go to the trouble of a face to face."

"You can go *in* now." The secretary added a secretive smile as I passed by.

"Jesus. Walker you could seduce a nun." Carlos opened the door.

"I don't need that particular sin on my hands. Anyway, she's no nun."

I stepped into the ultra-modern office. A mere five years older than me, Billings was the youngest owner in the league. He stood in front of a bank of floor-to-ceiling windows. Behind him the skyline of the city stretched out like a postcard. A huge desk made from half of a wing of a 747 took up the width of the space. Despite the owner's billions, Carlos dressed better. Hell, I dressed better. Billings looked like a college student in his jeans and "Geeks Shall Inherit the Earth" t-shirt.

"Hello, Mr. Billings." I was on my best behavior, though it went against my usual inclination to fight authority.

Out of the corner of my eye, I noticed we had an audience. I gave the two men, who had the bulk of my linemen, a cursory glance. A woman with dirt brown hair pulled back into a severe bun examined me, but not with any of the sexual interest that I was used to. Wearing a buttoned-up blouse underneath a boxy, sexless suit, she didn't pique my interest either. Was she purposely trying to look dowdy? Or was she trying to distract men from a pair of full lips that on second glance I wanted wrapped around my cock?

But she didn't look like she went in for that. And what good were lips that didn't smile? Probably as uptight in the bedroom as her hairstyle. Carlos gripped my shoulder, and I turned my attention back to my boss.

Billings pointed to two seats in front of the imposing desk. Was the size of the chairs a tactic our billionaire owner used to make his opponents feel powerless? I wished I felt as cool as Carlos looked. I relaxed back into the seat and mirrored my agent's pose.

"I'll get straight to the point, Walker. Yesterday, the front office received a death threat against you."

Was that all? I held in a sigh of relief about not being in trouble. I had more than my fair share of hate emails and tweets, and even a couple of death threats. Some were even funny.

Lost my Fantasy Football game by 4 points. That means 4 bullets to your balls. #deflatedballs

Seriously, people needed to get a life. But I took the good with the bad. It was just part of being a pro athlete.

One day they loved you and the next day they hated you. I didn't take it personally.

"Excuse me, but that's nothing new," I said.

"No, this is different." With a deep frown, Billings slid a sheet of paper across the wide expanse of the desk. "It's a color copy. The police have the original."

"The police?" If learning they were involved wormed a wiggle of doubt in my gut, then reading the words turned that wiggle into a brick. My heart slammed against the wall of my chest, then crashed to my stomach. In perfect precision, letters from newspapers and magazines headlines had been snipped and glued to the paper.

In DEATH we shall be ONE.

Soon, my LOVE. VERY, VERY soon.

XOXO

The word *Death* and the *XOXO* were in red.

Definitely not the typical threatening tweet or email. Groupies stalked me, but I couldn't remember any of them ever acting creepy or psychotic. None of my exes crossed my mind. Everyone knew what they were getting into based on my reputation off the field. No drama. No tears. No hearts broken.

Handing the paper to Carlos, I joked, "I'm guessing the x's and o's don't stand for offense and defense."

"This is serious, Dean."

I winced at the use of my first name. "Come on, someone is just fucking with me." I looked to the female. "Oh, sorry." I might be an arrogant fuck, but I didn't like to curse around women—except for dirty talk in the bedroom.

"No, the police have deemed the threat credible. The original letter is at the crime lab for DNA testing and fingerprinting." Billings nodded over to the two goons and the girl. "We've hired a security detail to protect you."

"Hell no." I shot up from my seat like I'd gotten sacked and I wanted to prove to the other team that I wasn't affected by the blow. I didn't want my teammates to think I was scared of a veiled threat on a piece of paper. I could take care of myself. "The only protection I need on the field is from my linemen, and off the field, a box of condoms will do."

A feminine snort sounded. I looked over in time to see the two men she was with glare at her.

As if guessing my concerns, Billings said, "Believe me, we don't want anyone knowing either. The fans might stay home and opposing teams will demand that you be sidelined. Oslo and Williams will be posing as equipment managers on the field. And off the field, Miss Reeves will—"

"What? Knit me a sweater?"

"As I was saying…" Billing gave me a look filled with warning. "Miss Reeves will be posing as your girlfriend."

"Just Reeves, sir."

"My girlfriend?" I couldn't help but laugh at the idea. "Sorry, baby doll, you are nothing like any of my girlfriends. No one will believe it. Not even with a makeover." I usually wasn't such an asshole, but she needed to think I was.

And oh boy, did I hit a nerve. Like a charging linebacker, Miss Uptight strode up with her light blue eyes shooting shards of ice. I had to give her credit though. The top of her head barely reached my chest yet she wasn't intimidated by my size.

She planted her fists firmly on her hips. The buttons on her blouse threatened to pop.

"Up here, buster." She pointed two fingers to her eyes. Though she talked tough, her voice was decidedly female. "I've gone undercover as a hooker, so there won't be a problem with people believing I'm your girlfriend."

I bit back a smile at her wit and instead gave a mocking smirk. But the image of her trying to fool some poor loser into a trick caused my brain to stutter. Not that my girlfriends looked like hookers. Slutty, oh yes. Easy, definitely yes. But I liked them that way.

I steered clear of the smart ones. A woman with brains like Miss Uptight was more dangerous than the woman who'd pasted together that threatening letter.

Still, I didn't want anyone to risk their life for me. And how was this mere slip of a girl supposed to protect me? It was insulting.

"I'm supposed to believe you'd take a bullet for me?"

"I haven't lost a man yet. But if you don't lose the attitude, I might make an exception."

A smart woman with a smart mouth. My gaze dropped to her lips. Pink and kissable. Soft. Unlike the rest of her. What did she wear underneath the sexless clothing? Granny panties? Or lingerie? Maybe she was the librarian type who kept a pair of red stilettos in her closet. Damn if I didn't want to find out.

"Miss Reeves is one of Ian's Worldwide Security and Investigators' finest."

I noted the wince on her face at the use of "miss" and I turned back to my boss, dismissing her. "And what am I supposed to do about getting laid?" Hopefully that would repulse Miss Uptight enough to make her flee the room.

I should have guessed she wouldn't be so easily deterred.

"Maybe if you wore a chastity belt and focused more on football instead of getting laid, you would have made the playoffs last year."

Now she'd struck a nerve. My team might be called the New York Kings, but we were second-class citizens to the city's darlings, the Cougars, who'd won last year's championship while I played golf. Which was why I'd been celibate since this season began. No more distractions. No more excuses.

Billings laughed. "Reeves, you handle Walker better than my head coach does."

Did the young billionaire get his kicks from seeing a female Secret Service wannabe give it to his quarterback? "What if I refuse?"

"If you don't cooperate, you'll be benched. Off the team. I'm serious. I'm responsible for you and your teammates. No player gets killed on my watch. This is just a game, for Christ's sake."

Football wasn't a game to me—it was life. It was the one thing that had connected my father to me, even more so now that he was dead. On the field I still felt his presence, cheering me on or offering advice. Off the field I felt adrift. Alone.

And even if Billings didn't admit it, I knew the game connected him to his own father too. I didn't need my psychology degree to know the only reason why Billings purchased the Kings was to impress his father. The geek son of a former hero of the gridiron had daddy issues.

"You're overreacting. It's not like this nut job knows where I live. The letter was sent to the office. Having a security detail will be a distraction to the team."

"Then if not for yourself, do it for your teammates and for the employees who work in this office that might get caught in the crossfire."

"Carlos?" I looked to my uncharacteristically silent agent for some backup.

"I'm sorry, Walker, but I have to agree with Billings."

Carlos held up the letter as if to remind me of the death threat, and my heart took a freefall to my gut again.

"It's in your best interest to comply," he continued.

Whose best interest? Carlos was only worried about his percentage. He couldn't make money off a dead quarterback.

I resigned myself to the security detail. But that didn't mean I couldn't come up with a game plan to rid me of Miss Uptight. "Looks like I'm stuck with you."

"Like Krazy Glue."

She might be the glue, but I would bring the crazy.

Chapter 2

Alexa Reeves

WHAT AN ASS.

I'd never met such an arrogant jerk. And in my line of business, I'd met plenty. Including my two muscle-head coworkers in the room with me. Of course, they weren't as attractive as the Kings' Quarterback.

Which made Dean Walker all the more infuriating. With his trim Van Dyke beard and sexy five o'clock shadow, he was hell sent with looks stolen from Satan himself. The high and tight cut of his black hair highlighted his handsome face, with slanted brows over whiskey eyes heady enough to drown your soul in. And a ripped body to shock you back to life. He was more of a legend off the field than on it.

He probably needed a bodyguard just to keep women from throwing themselves at him. I wondered how many he caught. And how many he threw back. Could his stalker be a rejected groupie? It was something to keep an eye on.

"Enjoy your last night of freedom," I said as I walked to the door. Though the thought of him tearing up the sheets with someone other than me bothered me more than it should have. I turned back before leaving. "Tomorrow you're officially off the market."

Dean blew me a kiss. I made a show of catching his sarcastic gesture, then flung it to the floor. But that didn't block the tingles of want from coursing through me. Stupid hormones. Maybe *I* needed to enjoy my last night of freedom before going head to head with football's most eligible bachelor.

God, what was wrong with me? I'd never been bitchy to a client. I was the pillar of professionalism. The tough-girl act wasn't planned, but it was clear when Dean entered the room that I had to establish from the get go that I wouldn't take his shit. I had to prove it to him, to his agent, and to the owner, who I suspected was gauging my ability to handle his moronic star.

Hell, I had to prove it to myself.

I left the room, leaving Oslo and Williams to take care of the details of tonight's watch with the rest of the security team. The secretary smiled and told me to have a nice day. She was Dean's type to a T. I grunted, "You, too."

Dean was right about one thing. I was nothing like the girls I'd seen him photographed with.

Not blonde enough, booby enough, girly enough,

sexy enough, and certainly not dumb enough.

As if I wanted to be any of those things.

But in less than twenty-four hours, I needed to trans-form myself from a rough and tumble bodyguard into a woman everyone could believe Dean Walker gave up his little black book for. This was a job for Joffrey Stars.

Joffrey had been dying to get his hands on me since junior high, where he went by Jeffery Sterling and I was his childhood protector. Now, as a stylist to the stars, he was more wealthy and famous than any of the kids who bullied us. Sending off a quick text, I wasn't surprised by his immediate response.

Hell hath surely frozen over.

I WALKED INTO Glamour Me, a one-stop makeover mecca, with indifference. This was a job. I wasn't doing this to impress the Kings' quarterback. I couldn't care less what he thought about me. This was just another assignment, I repeated. Upon closing the door and taking a few steps inside, the flowery smells mixed with chemicals assaulted my nose. The well-coifed hairstylists turned to gawk at me, and the buzz of the female chatter died down to a murmur.

My indifference turned to panic. Even though I was only five foot two, I felt like a bull in a china shop. I didn't belong here. Inadequate didn't begin to describe the way I felt. I decided to get the hell out before they could lay a hand on me. I turned to run.

"Oh no you don't," Joffrey shouted from the row of salon chairs. "Grab her."

The receptionist lunged for the door and spread her arms out like I was trying to escape from a mental ward. Except, I was the sane one. Who sits for hours at a time in order to impress someone? I had better things to do with my time.

"Damn it." I trudged over to Joffrey who led me to his private workspace in the back.

Dressed like a runway model, he was prettier than most women. If you passed him on the street, you wouldn't know he was born a male. Gender ambivalent, he could also rock a business suit when he felt like it. If he could transform himself, maybe there was hope for me.

"Let's get this over with." I plopped myself into the salon chair with a thud.

"A little more enthusiasm for my artistry, please."

"Sorry."

"Now, let me see what I have to work with. Hmm. You always had the nicest skin." Joffrey examined me like I was on the auction block, even lifting my upper lip. "Perfect teeth."

I smacked his hand away. "What am I, a horse?"

He ignored me, tilting my chin to the side. "Beautiful bone structure. You just need a little spit and polish."

"Oh my God, please tell me that is not some kind of new beauty treatment." Half serious and half joking, I knew women tried outrageous shit to keep the ravages of time at bay. From placenta facials to topically applied urine. No, thank you very much. I'd rather be an old hag.

Flicking a comb in his hand, Joffrey said, "Honey, if it worked, I'd be selling my own spit for hundreds of dollars a bottle."

He tugged at the bun on the top of my scalp until the mousy brown mane fell loose in a tumble of waves to the middle of my back. It was the only thing feminine about me. I should have cut it a long time ago. Long hair was a pain in the ass, hence the bun, but something always held me back. After this assignment, I was determined to embrace my height and go for a pixie cut.

"Honey, this is a rat's nest." He tugged the comb through the mass. "So why the change of heart? Please tell me it's over a man."

"No. A high-profile case where I need to be a client's arm candy."

"Who is it?"

As a stylist to the biggest names in Hollywood, Joffrey knew how to keep his lip zipped, so I owned up to my assignment. "I'm protecting Dean Walker."

"Oh, so it *is* over a man. And a yummy one at that. I am so jelly!"

"Don't be. I'm only pretending to be his girlfriend to keep close to him. So I need to look slutty, because that's his type."

"Girl, I don't do slutty. You don't want to be like all the rest. Make him see what he's missing."

"My job is to keep him alive, nothing more. So, I'm thinking… blonde?" I winced.

"Pfft, blonde is so cliché. No, we are going with salted caramel."

"I don't want him to eat my hair." I quirked a smile.

"By the time I'm done with you, he's going to want to devour you whole!"

My blood heated with the thought of Dean Walker's mouth on my skin. Would his beard tickle? Burn? Both?

We chatted about the people we knew in high school. Who was in jail… *Not surprised.* On drugs… *Again?* In rehab… *Again?* Going through a divorce… *What took her so long to dump him?*

Done with plastering my hair with dye and enough foils to channel radio signals from the other side of the universe, Joffrey asked, "Leg wax?"

Since I'd be wearing short skirts, I nodded. I didn't want to be shaving my legs everyday while on assignment. Being a woman sucked. Not that I wanted to be a man either. I guessed I was just as gender ambivalent as

Joffrey was. Maybe that was why we were such good friends. Yet I dated only men while Joffrey dated both sexes like he was choosing between coffee or tea.

"And a bikini wax?" He lowered his voice. "A Brazilian?" he added hopefully.

"No one will be seeing my vagina." I'd been too focused on my career to date, and Dean was strictly off-limits.

While I waited for aesthetician to prep my legs, I went over the list of potential suspects. Who wanted Dean Walker dead? The possibilities were endless. A rejected groupie, a past girlfriend, a fan, someone the quarterback had pissed off?

When the first strip was ripped off, *I* wanted to kill Dean myself for making me want to look the part. I was ready to hop off the table when another strip was ripped away. Fuck, that hurt! And women did this to their vagina?

Once that was done, I was off to a makeup lesson. I could take down a guy twice my size and hit a target with my gun from fifty yards, but makeup application took a different skill set. Joffrey's assistant had power shopped in the meantime, bringing me a wardrobe complete with accessories. Using my phone, I took a picture of each outfit so I wouldn't forget the look.

Three long hours later, Joffrey backed away. "Another masterpiece!"

After being prodded, plucked, and waxed, I was ready for my reveal. With an eye roll worthy of a teenage girl, I slid off the chair without any great expectations. That way the disappointment of me still being me wouldn't sting.

I gazed into the full-length mirror and blinked. That was me?

No, it couldn't be. That woman was sexy. Pretty. The only hint of myself in the woman staring back at me was in the eyes. My expression was one of shock and awe.

Standing behind me, Joffrey fussed with my hair. "See how the deep brunette color makes your light blue eyes pop and the soft caramel highlights combined with the cut, frames your heart-shaped face. You look like an angel."

The effect did create a mirage of softness that I never thought possible. But an angel? I held back a snort.

"OMG." The receptionist peeked in. "Why do you hide that hourglass figure underneath that hideous suit you walked in here wearing? You look ten pounds thinner!"

"Francine!" Joffrey admonished. "We do not insult the clientele about their fashion faux pas." Turning back to me, he added, "Sorry, Alexa, she's new."

"No, that suit *was* hideous, and she made up for it by telling me I look ten pounds thinner." I was happy about the compliment. What woman wouldn't be? See, I was already turning into one of them!

But the light blue pencil skirt with dark blue polka dots did hug my tiny waist, and the blue blouse revealed a hint of cleavage that had never seen the light of day. The thick heels were a reasonable three inches in height, but I doubted I'd be able to chase down an assailant if I had to. Maybe with some practice I'd learn.

Holy crap. Maybe I could pull this off.

Now, would I be taken seriously? This job would prove to Ian that I could handle a high-profile case. And that I had what it took to protect a man. "Where am I going to hide my gun?"

Tossing me a matching light blue jacket, Joffrey said, "I had a pocket sewn in. Denise is working on the rest of the clothing."

Along with my concealment undergarments, which would hide a smaller gun, I'd be packing heat like I normally did. "You're the best fairy godmother a body-guard could have."

"Ha! Cinderella was lucky I wasn't her fairy god-mother. This queen would have stolen her prince."

I laughed. "Believe me, Dean Walker is no prince."

"Well, if I can turn you from ho-hum to a hubba-hubba in a day, you can turn Walker from a frog to a prince."

"That's not in the job description. I'm only supposed to protect the frog not kiss it." Still, I wondered what

Dean would think when he saw my transformation, and I hated myself for it.

Joffrey popped another button on my blouse and adjusted my boobs to show more cleavage than I was comfortable with. "Mixing business with pleasure is not a crime."

But according to Ian's Security's employee handbook it *was* against the rules. A bodyguard should never get involved with the body they were protecting. The employees with a dick, however, broke the rule all the time. Everyone, including me, turned a blind eye to it. But as a woman, it would end my career. It was unfair, but unfair didn't matter in the real world.

"And would it kill you to smile?"

"It might." But I risked death and smiled anyway. "Thank you." I kissed Joffrey on the cheek. "I love it. Please send the clothes to my apartment. The bill goes to Ian's Worldwide Security. Add a nice tip for everyone who helped me."

Mastering the three-inch heels would take some time, but I walked out of Glamour Me with a lot more confidence than I did going in.

I might not be a blonde bombshell, but Dean Walker was about to be blindsided.

Chapter 3

Dean

WHO THE HELL was knocking at my door at 7:00 a.m.? Normally, I'd be in bed with a smoking, curvy body snaked around me. Instead I'd become the fucking poster boy for celibacy. Horny as hell, I was not in a good mood. I whipped the door open, ready to take my frustration out on whoever was on the other side.

A barrel of a gun stared back at me. What the fuck? You would think my quick reflexes on the field would serve me off it. In this case they didn't.

"Bang, bang, you're dead," quipped Reeves. My bodyguard smirked as she lowered her gun. "The security in this building sucks. I swept right by the doorman. And if you bothered to check the peephole, you wouldn't be shitting in your Superman boxers right now."

She breezed by, rolling a large suitcase behind her. Half naked, I just stood there, thunderstruck. Because of how Reeves looked with her hair down or because of the gun, I couldn't say—or admit to.

Turning my head as she passed, I detected a slight wobble in her gait, from the heels no doubt. Still, her ass had a sexy sway in the body-hugging skirt. And what a body she had. Why did she hide those curves underneath boxy suits? Criminal. Hitting just above the knee, there was nothing criminal about the length of her skirt. She rocked it like that chick from *Madmen,* and somehow it was way hotter than a miniskirt.

Parking the suitcase by the end table, she turned and slid the gun inside her blazer, like it was a wallet instead of a weapon.

She was a walking contradiction. Was I more turned on by the way she handled the gun or by her cleavage beckoning me to suffocate myself in it? And those lips, now enhanced with a red gloss, made my morning hard-on roar back with a vengeance.

She looked soft. Touchable. But the look was lost in translation when it came to her body language. With her hands on her hips, she was as tough as the steel of the gun she carried. "Are you going to shut the door or what?"

Fuck. Pissed that she'd caught me off guard in more ways than one—seriously, I was wearing the Superman boxers my nephew gave me for Christmas last year—I slammed the door and walked toward her. I didn't have a problem with guns, but guilt by association could, at the very least, land me a fine with the league. "The gun laws in the city are strict. Am I going to get in trouble if you get caught?"

"The employees of Ian's Security have special licenses to carry concealed weapons."

"Do you have more guns on you?"

"Now where else would I be packing?" She opened up her arms revealing a tiny waist that I bet my hands could span.

"Hmm." I leisurely eyeballed her from toe to head. She certainty didn't look like a bodyguard. The transformation from yesterday was astonishing. From GI Jane to Tinker Bell sexpot. "Nowhere that I can see. Maybe I should frisk you?"

"You could try." Her smile was more of a smirk, daring me to do exactly that.

Oh yeah, Reeves was wrestle-you-to-the-ground sexy. But I preferred a bed. "Since you're obviously not here to take care of this…" I pointed to the tent in my boxers. "Why exactly are you here? And what's with the suitcase?"

Dropping her gaze, she arched an eyebrow, then looked back up to meet my eyes. "I'll be living here and driving you to practice each day like a dutiful girlfriend."

This was getting interesting. Still, having her around all the time would be a mix of inconvenience and temptation. "I only have one bed. And I'm not sleeping on the couch."

"I'm taking the couch. It has a perfect view of the front door."

She was hardcore. I took a step closer. "What if I said I'd feel safer if you were in bed with me?"

"Let's get something straight. I'm your bodyguard, not a body you're going to be banging."

"That's too bad. You have a banging hot body." I took another step. Close enough to kiss her. Her beautiful light blue eyes rimmed with gray widened, but she didn't back away.

"Hot enough that your friends will believe us as a couple?"

"No."

"Oh."

The wounded look in her eyes punched me in the gut. I was a total bastard for playing her like this. "You don't look like a hooker."

The beginnings of a smile lifted at the corners of her luscious mouth. "Consider me an upgrade." She backed away, dismissing me.

This was going to be tougher than I thought. I couldn't take my eyes off her ass as she strode to the window in full bodyguard mode. The urge to hike up the tight skirt to her hips and bend her over the couch hit me hard. She pushed open the curtains, yanking me out of my fantasy. The sunlight blasted in, reminding me that I had to get to practice.

"Nice view," she said without turning around.

"Thanks." It cost a pretty penny, a lot of pretty pennies. I loved New York City, but the energy could be draining. Up here, I felt like I wasn't living in the city.

Her hand swept the skyline. "There's no line of sight."

"As in a sniper?" I shook my head. "Aren't you taking this a little too seriously?"

"Aren't you taking it a lot too lightly?"

Yeah, this was going to be a lot tougher than I thought. With the way she blocked, she could be on my offensive line.

"Maybe," I conceded.

"I'll need your phone." She held out her hand.

"Why?"

"I need to check your texts, emails, and photos for any suspicious activity that you might have ignored or thought unimportant. My team has already gone through your social-media accounts, tracking back three months. And I also need your schedule for the coming week. And a key to the apartment."

This was starting to get a little too real for me. I'd shrugged off yesterday's meeting and hadn't given a second thought to the death threat until I answered the door with a gun to my face as my wakeup call.

"The schedule is no problem, but my phone is private. I have sensitive information on it." The thought of giving her or any woman a key turned my stomach.

She snorted, which actually sounded kind of cute. "Sensitive my ass. Look, we can do this the easy way."

"Or?"

"I can hack my way in."

"Christ." Fine. Let her read the sex texts and see the naked pictures chicks sent to me on a daily basis. Maybe she'd be shocked enough to quit. Who would want to protect someone like me anyway? "It's on the coffee table." The alarm from my bedroom blared. "The code is thirteen-thirteen. I have to get ready for practice."

I took a quick shower, taking care of my hard-on in record speed, fantasizing about Reeves's sassy and luscious mouth doing the work instead of my hand, while she was in the next room scrolling through naked picture after naked picture of other women.

She was swiping the screen with her thumb when I walked out of my bedroom dressed in khaki pants and a black polo shirt. Smiling, I wondered what she would say if I told her that we had been intimate in my shower.

"Oh, this is so just too good to be true. Priceless." Reeves barked out a laugh.

When she flicked her fingers for the zoom function, I became curious to what she was looking at. I crooked my head to see the screen. *Shit.* An old photo of my junk took up the whole viewing area. I thought I'd deleted it after sending it to an actress I'd been dating. I made a grab for the phone, but I wasn't quick enough.

"Oh come on, it's not like hundreds of women haven't seen it before."

"Not hundreds." Why did it bother me that she came across the dick pic, when just five minutes ago I'd been fantasying about her mouth swallowing me whole?

"What's the problem? You're obviously proud of it." She paused, tapping the phone on her chin. "Or is not yours?" She arched an eyebrow.

"It's mine. I was drunk."

Reeves laughed, and while I loved the throaty sound, I hated that it was at my expense. I hoped she was laughing at my stupidity and not at my dick. Why did I even fucking care what her opinion of it was or her general opinion of me?

"Next time use Snapchat." She smacked the phone to my chest and let go before walking away. I fumbled but caught it before it hit the floor. "And using the number of your jersey as a security code is dumber than one of your blonde bimbos."

Fuck. What the hell was going on? Worst-case scenario, my bad boy behavior would cause her to quit. Best-case, she'd fall into my bed and be forced to resign. Yet here she was lecturing me like I was some hormonal teenager. For some reason that's exactly how I felt around her.

It had been so long since I'd had to work at getting a

girl that I was clearly out of practice. I'd have to put in some overtime to get Reeves on my team.

And what the hell was her first name?

Chapter 4

Alexa

WHAT AN ASS. *But what a penis.*

The shock of coming across the photo of his privates had quickly turned to interest, then to throbbing want. I needed to be away from him and the image of what he packed inside his form-fitting khakis—and oh, the good lord, those Superman boxers he'd worn earlier. More like Supercock.

I escaped to tour the apartment to determine if there were any security issues to be addressed.

Thanks to building safety codes, windows up this high were not made to be opened. Sleek and modern, the living room lacked warmth, which didn't surprise me. Dean was about as warm and fuzzy as a porcupine. The dining room and kitchen looked unused. I took a quick peek inside the fridge. A box of five dozen eggs, multiple containers from a local health food caterer, and a six-pack of beer took up the space. Looked like I'd be ordering in for the duration of my stay.

I headed to the hallway to search the rest of the apartment.

"I'm leaving in five minutes," Dean notified me as I passed by him. "I'll text my agent to send you my schedule."

"I need that key," I instructed over my shoulder. Was he checking out my ass? My heel slid on the floor as I transitioned from carpet to the marble tile, and I stumbled.

"Careful, it's slippery."

"Thank you, Captain Obvious." Before he could make a stinging comeback, I ducked into the first room off the hallway. The second bedroom had been converted into a state-of-the-art gym. A few trophies lined a shelf, and a hall of fame of photos hung on the wall. While I was glad I'd be able to get in my workouts, I'd be surrounded by Dean's image. Dean with famous athletes. Dean with celebrities. Dean. Dean. Dean.

I lingered longer than I should have, putting off the recon of his bedroom. Would it be as sterile as the rest of the house or as virile as his body promised?

I turned to leave, but Dean blocked the exit, placing his hands on either side of the doorframe. A key dangled from one of his fingers. He smelled clean with a hint of spice and leather. The scent tickled my nose and other places that hadn't felt a tingle in months. The biceps that powered long passes stretched the fabric of the short-sleeved polo shirt as he flexed. Underneath, I knew his six-pack abs were honed to a chiseled work of art worthy of a special exhibit in a museum.

Oslo and Williams were broader and meatier than Dean, but my coworkers didn't make me feel small. Like a female. Like a woman.

I hated how weak I felt around him. I couldn't let on how much he affected me. "Excuse me," I said sharply.

"Now is that a nice way to talk to your boyfriend?"

"Pretty please," I said with none of the sweetness the phrase called for.

"Not feeling it. Tell me your first name and I'll let you pass."

Dean's satanic smile created a sinful thrum through my body. "Why?"

"I like to be on a first-name basis with women who have seen my dick."

I would have laughed, but his feathery touch on my cheek caused every bone in my body to melt. I caught myself before I stepped closer to him.

"And as your boyfriend, I can't be calling you by your last name."

"Pretend boyfriend," I sputtered. "Pretend," I repeated, more to remind myself than to remind him.

"Of course. But we each have a role to play." Dean placed the key in my hand, then trailed a finger over my wrist. "You look the part, but can you act like my girlfriend?"

"All in a day's work," I said with more bravado than I felt. What the hell was wrong with me? Dean was a client. Protecting him was an assignment, not a chance to act out a role-playing fantasy of quarterback and cheerleader. As if I ever wanted to be a cheerleader.

"You know as my *pretend* girlfriend, you'll have to pretend to like me?"

That wouldn't be the problem at all. I liked him. Well, not like, but lust. Oh hell, yes. Lots and lots of lust. And I could blame the blush in my cheeks and my googly eyes on my acting skills. "It will take an Academy Award winning performance."

"And the Oscar goes to…?"

I bit my lip. *Just tell him. It's just a name.* My reluctance was bordering on cowardice, and I hated being a coward. "Alexa."

"Alexa." His voice lowered, husky yet with a touch of velvety smoothness. Seductive. "It suits you. Beautiful and tough."

Beautiful? Now who was acting? And he had to be acting. But his eyes mirrored my want.

"Um, don't you have to be at practice?" Please, anywhere or anything just to get away from his dominating presence.

I should have backed away, but I wouldn't let him win this little power play. From an early age I'd acted bigger than my size. I was fearless, but he made me afraid. Not in the physical sense, but on an emotional level that was as foreign to me as the clothes I was wearing.

"Yes, I do." He leaned in. "You make a man forget himself."

He wasn't the only one who was forgetting themselves. I was his bodyguard, not his lover, yet the desire to meet him the rest of the way for the kiss he was teasing me for almost overwhelmed me. But that's all it was, a tease. Worse yet, a test. Oh, God. What if his come-on was some elaborate plan to put me in a compromising position?

I laughed and threw in a snort. "Seriously, Dean, who falls for those kind of lines?"

Dropping his other hand from the doorframe, he dragged his fingers through his short hair. "Fuck, let's go."

I was relieved when he gave up first because I was one breath away from giving in, of crossing that line and kissing him into a state of amnesia. Before leaving, I texted the security team that we were on the move. The recon of his bedroom would have to wait.

We rode in silence down the elevator. I reveled in the stillness, knowing once we hit the street I was going to have a fight on my hands when he found out that I was also his driver.

Raising a brow, Dean mockingly bowed as he held the door. I swept by since I needed to be ahead of him to watch out for anything suspicious as we left the building. I tapped my ear as an *all okay* signal to Dubois, who was watching from a surveillance van.

We dashed across the one-way street to the multi-level garage, but I placed myself between him and any car that might screech out from a parking space.

Walking right by his Porsche, I said, "Our ride is this way."

Dean stopped. "Mine will be faster."

"Is it bulletproof?"

"No."

"Then we take my vehicle."

He obediently followed, but said, "Give me the keys."

"Did you train with the CIA?"

"The Culinary Institute?"

"Don't be an ass."

"Come on, that was funny."

I hit the remote for the locks and engine starter as we approached Ian's Security's pimped-out Cadillac Escalade, surprised that I didn't get more of an argument when I climbed behind the wheel.

I darted in and out of the traffic, checking the rear-view mirror from time to time for a possible tail.

"Will you slow the fuck down?"

"And you said your Porsche would be faster. Hah."

"I wasn't aware I'd be driving with Danica Patrick."

"It's called evasive driving." Okay, so I was driving a little erratically, but I needed the distraction to get his dick pic out of my brain. The fact that I was in charge of protecting a guy who took pictures of his genitals should have disgusted me. Instead I was disgusted with myself for dwelling on it—for being utterly fascinated by it.

I cut off a cab and shot between two busses.

"Jesus, I thought you were supposed to protect me, not kill me."

"Don't be such a drama queen." I smiled, but I slowed up a bit. "We need to work on our cover story."

"What do you mean?" Dean relaxed into his seat.

"How we met, for starters."

"Strip club?"

I gave him a side-eyed glance. "Too cliché."

"Bible study?"

I didn't take my eyes off the road, but I could actually feel his smile.

"Now that would really ruin your reputation, wouldn't it?" I took the turn for the tunnel out of the city. His deep laughter rumbled through the SUV and through my body. In the darkness of the tunnel, I shifted in my seat. "Let's keep it simple," I said.

Dean stroked his beard. "I know. We'll say my sister introduced us."

"Trudy in California?"

"Jesus. How do you—never mind."

He wouldn't be happy to find out I had a dossier on Dean Walker that would impress the FBI. We spent the rest of the way going over the cover story.

He directed me to the players parking area, and I pulled up to the curb by the entrance. I notified Oslo of our arrival, and he gave me the all clear.

"What are you going to be doing while I'm at practice?" asked Dean.

"I didn't take you for a controlling boyfriend."

"Whoa, I'm not…" Then he noticed my smile. "You should do that more often."

"Smile?"

"Yes, it makes you look…"

Pretty?

"…human," he said.

Oh. "I'll pick up you after practice. Oslo or Williams will text me."

"Don't I get a kiss goodbye?"

His eyes were full of mischief, but just the thought of his lips on mine created mayhem inside my body.

"No need. Nobody is looking." *Thank God.* I didn't think I was quite ready for that part of the act.

"Couldn't hurt to practice," he teased. Or maybe he wasn't.

"I think we both know you don't need any practice."

I tried to keep my tone light, even though sarcasm burned on the tip of my tongue.

"What about you? Do you need practice? A rehearsal?"

I shook my head. "Just two pair of lips coming together. No big deal."

"Baby doll, then you haven't been properly, or rather improperly, kissed."

"If you call me that one more time, it's not your stalker you're going to need protection from." I hated that I was a fraud. The endearment, said with hint of roughness, sweetly echoed inside me. And if he kissed me any which way, I'd turned the SUV around and head back to his apartment. Hell, I'd drag him into the backseat.

"God, you're sexy when you talk tough." Dean opened the car door and got out, turning to wink at me before going into the players entrance.

He was sexy standing still. How the hell was I suppose to watch out for threats when I could barely keep my eyes off of Dean?

Chapter 5

Dean

PUTTING THE DEATH threat out of my mind was a hell of a lot easier than banishing Alexa from my thoughts.

Pint-sized and mouthy, the bodyguard wasn't my type at all, yet I couldn't think of any other woman I'd rather take to bed tonight. Or take on any one of the pieces of my gym equipment. If she'd given me the slightest encouragement earlier, I would have gotten her out of my system on the weight bench that beckoned behind her as we stood in the doorway of my home gym. But there had been no encouragement, only annoyance.

Either she was immune to my charms or I was losing my touch.

I threw a half-assed pass to my wide receiver, Nicolai Ward. When the ball landed five feet in front of him, he stood with his hands in the air as if to say, *What the fuck was that?*

Coming back to the huddle, he ribbed, "Get your

head out of your ass, Walker."

"I can't help it if my ass is that cute," I quipped.

"It's not, white boy."

"Glad to hear that *you* think so, but the ladies beg to differ. And I do mean beg."

"Beg you to stop."

"Your sister didn't," I joked with a wide smile.

"Damn," said Parker, my running back. The offensive linemen hooted.

"You don't have the balls to go after my sister. You'd be a dead man, and I'd be talking to a ghost right now."

Dead man. If Ward only knew how close I was to dying for real. That is, if you took the threat seriously, which I didn't.

Before we could run another play, the whistle blew, and the head coach called me over. Oslo, posing as one of the equipment managers, handed off a water bottle, and I took a long drink.

The coach waited until Oslo made himself scarce, then said, "I've been advised of your situation."

Fuck. The last thing I needed was my coach questioning my ability to lead the team. "It's nothing. Billings is overreacting."

"This is not going to distract you?"

"No way. You can count on me. Besides, it's a bunch of bullshit."

"Well, if I haven't killed you yet..." The coach let

the comment hang.

"Aww, coach, you hurt my feelings." With my antics off the field, I would bet he had thought of murder, but come game day, I was the one he wanted in the pocket. I might not have the best arm in the league, but I had the best mind for football, reading the opposing team's defense like tomorrow's sports pages.

Nobody wanted to win more than me—nobody took a loss harder than me. Missing the playoffs last year for the first time in my eight-season career had hurt. I hadn't nursed my wounds so much as I'd fed them, working my ass off during the off-season. This was the year the Kings would rule NYC. This was the year we would go to the championship game and win that almighty ring. Shut the damn media up and make all the haters eat leather. I'd earn my paycheck, and then Carlos would negotiate for more when my contract was up at the end of year. Bigger endorsement deals. More women.

At eight and two, the team could smell the playoffs, but with the Washington Warriors breathing down our necks at seven and three, there was no room for distractions. No room for death threats and none for a cute little bodyguard who gave as good as she got. She'd surprised me. I needed to draw up another game plan. I had to stop messing around. Let Alexa do her job and I'd do mine. Fucking win it all.

The rest of practice ran smoothly. I hit my targets,

and I was feeling pleased with myself as my teammates and I headed for the exit.

As promised, Alexa was waiting for me by the door, looking good enough to lick.

"Hey, baby doll." What happened to my decision not to mess with her? But I couldn't help myself. The flash of anger in her eyes was like a sweet rush to my blood.

"Baby doll?" questioned Parker.

"What do we have here?" asked Ward, who was eye-balling my bodyguard. "Why, aren't you the little pocket rocket."

Pocket rocket? That was the perfect description of Alexa. Crap, I hadn't anticipated how my teammates would react. "This is Alexa, my girlfriend."

"Girlfriend? You?" asked Parker.

The way he said it was like I was incapable of a relationship. "Don't act so shocked. Quarterbacks need love too."

Parker, Ward, and two of my linemen gathered around Alexa like she was a shiny new toy. "Are you a porn star?" Parker asked, starting the inquisition.

"That would be a negative," she answered. Being surrounded by four oversized males would have intimidated any other woman, but Alexa stood her ground.

"Stripper?" asked Jacobs, my center.

Alexa gave me a side-eyed glance before responding

with another negative.

"Acrobat?" guessed Tony, my left guard.

"I know, I know," butted in Ward. "An Olympic gymnast!"

My teammates didn't know when to let up.

"Cut it out, guys." I put my arm around Alexa, staking my claim.

The sudden feel of the soft curve of her hip against my thigh jolted my dormant protective instincts to the surface. She was the one who was supposed to be guarding me, but it didn't sit right. I was all for women's rights—my two sisters not only were great moms, but they crushed it in the corporate world. However, when it came to physical threats, it was a man's job—no, it was his duty—to protect his woman. Maybe, this was what I was feeling—a natural instinct to protect what was mine, even if it was pretend.

There was no threat from my teammates, other than their own natural instinct to hit on a pretty girl. From the way Alexa blocked me, I knew she'd handle these bozos with ease. Unfortunately, she did it at my expense.

She shook her head. "Not even close, boys. I'm a dominatrix."

Holy crap. If only she was. Wait, maybe she was. The way she barked out orders, Alexa might be. I didn't know if this turned me on or not, but I was definitely curious.

My teammates thought the idea was hilarious.

Whether it was because of Alexa's tiny stature or because they knew my playboy lifestyle didn't mesh with a controlling female, I couldn't say, but I did know that by tomorrow there'd be whips, chains, and ball-gags decorating my locker. *Fuck.*

"She's an accountant," I said, sticking to the story we'd created.

"Yeah, by day." Alexa flirted, smiling at my team like a femme fatale from a James Bond movie.

Oh, holy hell. Why didn't I get to see that side of her? And why did a pang of jealousy gnaw at me like I was her real boyfriend?

Then she smacked my ass hard. Harder than I thought a girl of her size could muster.

"Come on, big boy," said Alexa. "Let's get you home where you belong."

I was one part humiliated and a whole-hell-of-a-lot turned on.

The quicker we got to the SUV, the less time they would have to ask questions or leer at her as if she were a delectable morsel to be gobbled up.

I steered her toward the parking lot and away from the pack mentality of my bros. "Why did you say that?"

"I was worried they weren't buying me as your girl-friend." Alexa hit the locks of the SUV and got in.

I slid into the passenger seat beside her. "It had nothing to do with you and everything to do with me. I'm not exactly boyfriend material."

"For a moment you had me fooled."

"You're not the only one who can give an Oscar-worthy performance." I wished it had been an act. My protectiveness must have been some deeply ingrained male DNA, like a fight-or-flight response to danger. Alexa triggered something primal in me, deeper than my normal drive to have wild sex.

She drove the speed limit, adhering to the traffic laws. The ride back to the city was uneventful except for the constant pinging of texts, which I knew were from my teammates. I put the phone on silent so I could decompress from the day of drills, and oh yeah, from having a gun pointed in my face.

At my apartment I obediently waited inside by the door while she went room to room like an episode of *Law and Order.* That nagging wrongness of letting a female protect me returned. I was the one who should check for intruders. Kill spiders, and shit like that.

"All clear."

I headed for the fridge and took out a prepared meal, popping it in the microwave. "Hungry?" I called out.

"I just ordered a pizza."

I poked my head out. "A little thing like you is going to eat a whole pizza?"

"No, I'll save some for breakfast. I like it cold."

"That's disgusting."

"So is humping every vagina over eighteen."

"I love it when you talk dirty."

I carried a plate filled with grilled chicken and vegetables past my unused dining room and plopped my tired body onto the leather couch. Before digging in, I switched on the state-of-the-art smart TV and downloaded some game film to review. I never showed up to a game unprepared, watching and analyzing hours of footage the team prepared at my request. I knew the other team's defense inside and out. It gave me the edge over the other quarterbacks in the league that failed to realize the importance of knowing your enemy. Talent only got you so far in the pros.

Behind me Alexa paced, driving me a little nuts. She was a ball of energy that couldn't be contained, always seeming to be in motion.

"Why don't you grab us a couple of beers, baby doll?"

I felt her stop at the back my head. "Excuse me? I'm not your maid."

Risking certain death, I turned my head to gaze up at her with a confused expression. "But you are my girlfriend," I joked.

She put her hands on her hips. "Of all the sexist—"

The buzz of intercom saved me from a rant on how I was a male pig. It was my own fault for giving her plenty of ammunition. I couldn't understand my need to provoke her or the satisfaction it gave me to see her cheeks flush with anger.

I bent my head back and saw Alexa at the door, gun in hand, peering through the peephole. Seemingly satisfied that the pizza-delivery guy was not a serial killer, she put the gun in the waistband of her skirt, opened the door and paid the man.

She dropped the box on my clean coffee table, threw open the lid, grabbed a slice, and folded it like a true New Yorker.

"I do have plates." I said as she took a bite.

"Yeah, but then I'd have to clean it up," she mumbled with her mouth half full.

She had a point. I hadn't had pizza in months and the aroma wafted in the air, more seductive than any perfume.

Fuck it. "Can I have a slice?"

"If you go get us some beers."

The little minx had what only could be described as a cat-who-just-ate-the-canary grin. And damn if I didn't want to forgo the pizza and take a bite out of her instead.

By the time I got back with the beers and some plates, she'd taken off her blazer and the gun rested on the end table. I didn't know whom I liked more, the fake Alexa, dressed to kill, or the real Alexa, who downed a beer like a guy and would tell me to fuck off in an instant.

Alexa nodded to the screen. "You're playing the Seattle Steelheads on Sunday?"

"Yeah." We talked football, and I was surprised to find out she knew more than the basics.

"Any inside tips for my Fantasy Football team?"

"That would be unethical." Not that I would complain if Alexa turned unethical all over me with her smoking body. "Who did you draft as your quarterback?"

She hesitated. "McQueen."

Playing for the NY Cougars, he was my enemy on the field. It hurt that I wasn't her choice, even if McQueen did win the championship last year. But did the jealousy I feel go deeper than that?

"He's a pussy." I took a swig of beer.

"All quarterbacks are pussies," she teased.

Her throaty laughter had me thinking of her pussy. With her gun inches away, I decided it was safer to concentrate on the screen. I winced when Dawson, the Steelheads' defensive back, pummeled the quarterback from the Washington Warriors into the ground so hard that it left an impression in the muddy field.

"Ouch," said Alexa. "I guess you quarterbacks are tougher than you look."

Having her around wasn't as bad as I thought it would be. I actually enjoyed her company. I enjoyed it too much. Most of the conversations I'd had with women in the last couple of years had gone like this: *My place or yours?* followed by *Oh, yes, Dean, yes. Oh God, yes.* Or some variation of that.

Tired from the day of practice, the carbs from the pizza, and the buzz of the beer, my eyes started to close. "I'm calling it a night. There are blankets in the hall closet."

"Thanks."

I got up and headed for the hallway, then turned around. Alexa had already inspected the apartment, but I still asked. "Sure you don't want to check for monsters under the bed?"

"The only monster in your room is—"

"In my pants," I finished her sentence.

Shaking her head, she tossed a throw pillow at me. "Down boy."

Easier said than done, but I behaved and went to bed alone and aching.

Chapter 6

Alexa

WHO WAS THE woman staring back from Dean's guest bathroom mirror? It wasn't me, it couldn't be. But it was. In a little over a week I'd devolved from a woman who didn't wear makeup to one who knew the pros and cons of powder versus liquid foundation. I wasn't certain if I liked my reflection, but I knew I didn't like the way it made me feel. Like a woman. Vulnerable. And that was not in my job description.

Joffrey had gone a little overboard with the makeup, but he had insisted that tonight's venue called for drama. The cat-eyed look included false eyelashes, which felt like little spiders on my eyelids. He had styled my hair in messy waves so I wouldn't have to fuss with it during the evening, he said. Like I ever fussed with my hair.

He'd had me try on a little black dress at first, and I did mean little—short and one size too small, clinging to every curve like it had been poured onto my skin. I had struggled out of it, claiming there was no way I could conceal a gun, which was true, but it had more to do with me being uncomfortable displaying my body to the whole world.

Now, clothed in a blush-colored V-neck sweater dress with bronze sequins sprinkled through the fabric, I looked like a rocker princess. The hem was still short, but the fit was loose enough to allow for the gun-concealment compression midriff tank I wore underneath.

In three-inch wedge-heeled brown leather sandals, I could barely feel myself walk. How was I supposed to feel the gas pedal? The shoes matched the thick belt cinched at my waist, and according to Joffrey, style won over safety every time.

I didn't agree. In an act of fashion defiance, I changed into the leather cowboy booties I'd packed when I moved in with Dean.

I fisted my hand, pleased with the large bronze flower ring on my finger. The jewelry was more dangerous than a set of brass knuckles, though I was sure that was not what Joffrey had in mind when he'd selected the ring. I slid my gun into the sewn in holster via the V neck of the dress and then I practiced drawing. The bell sleeves could trip me up, so I drew a few more times.

Satisfied that I would not have a wardrobe malfunction, I took a deep breath to calm my nerves. Martini Madness was the hottest club in New York City, and if that wasn't enough to make me break out in hives, then the charity event, bringing in every celebrity in town, would. Not only was this a logistical nightmare for a bodyguard, I had to look and act like I belonged in that world, to fit in with the "it" crowd. And I never fit in.

Except, Joffrey had worked his magic like my own personal fairy godmother.

I took one last look in the mirror. "You can do this," I said to my reflection.

Enough dawdling. My date—correction, my *assignment*—waited in the living room. I opened the door, but halted when I heard Joffrey and Dean's voice drifting down the hall.

I smiled, picturing Joffrey fussing with Dean's tie as if we were off to the senior prom instead of a nightclub. To Dean's credit, he hadn't blinked an eye when Joffrey, in all his glory, had swept into the apartment to help me get ready. I'd been afraid the macho athlete would hurt Joffrey's feelings with an off-color remark. Dean took the chaos in his apartment in stride.

Now I heard whispering. In stealth mode, I crept closer.

"I see how you look at Alexa. She's my dearest friend. If you hurt her—"

"Understood." Dean cut him off, not laughing at Joffrey's pretense of toughness or questioning what he meant by how Dean "looked at" me.

I wished he would ask because I would like to know.

"How long have you been friends?" asked Dean instead.

Like someone spilling their guts to a tabloid gossip columnist, Joffrey divulged how I stuck up for him in school, fighting his fights and my own until the bullies went on to easier targets.

"But don't let that fool you. I've since taken self-defense classes and I'm not afraid to return the favor."

I decided it was time to join the fray. Stepping into the living room, my heart stopped and my libido started. The black-on-black suit was tailored to Dean's perfect body. How could he be so sexy with clothes on? It wasn't fair. He was fiddling with the cufflinks when he raised his gaze, his eyes heating like whiskey set on fire, and I burned along with him. A wicked smile appeared on his face, as if he were Satan come to claim my soul and along with it, my heart.

"See that, right there. That's the look I'm talking about. Like you're the wolf and Alexa is Little Red Riding Hood."

Before I could scold Joffrey, Dean laughed. "Yeah, except she carries a gun in her basket."

"And don't you forget it," said Joffrey, pointing a finger at Dean. Then he crooked his digit at me. "And you, little missy, don't think I didn't notice you changed shoes. Where do you think you're going—a hoedown?

Come with me."

I followed him into the guest bathroom and waited until he closed the door.

I folded my arms. "What happened between yesterday and now? Then you wanted me to throw myself at him, and now you're acting like my overprotective brother."

"Because after I saw how you looked at him, I realized it would be more than a roll in the hay for you."

"You need your eyes checked, Joffrey." There was no way I was mooning over Dean with anything other than lust. He was a client. An assignment. And if Dean wanted me, he wanted this version of me, not the woman he'd met in his boss' office. I needed to remember that. Thankfully Joffrey forgot all about my cowboy booties.

I was mulling Joffrey's claim as I drove to the club, when Dean broke the uncomfortable silence.

"I didn't get the chance to say, but you look delicious."

Being a star quarterback, Dean Walker had his pick of beautiful women. Where did I fall on his scale? I hated myself for wondering. Hated that I didn't know how to react to his compliment. On the outside I might look different, but I was still the same me on the inside.

Awkward and unsure, I said, "I bet you say that to all your bodyguards."

His deep laughter rumbled through my body.

"Certainly not to Oslo and Williams."

I laughed too, stopping just before I snorted. It was a terrible habit I was trying to break. I rarely laughed and when I did, the sound of it surprised me, causing me to snort.

I pulled up behind the line of cars, limos, and SUVs waiting for the valet. A sea of celebrities flooded into Martini Madness. I was hesitant to give up my keys. Not having the means of a quick escape concerned me, but I had no choice. I pushed the on button to my earpiece and spoke with my team, who confirmed everything was in place in case we needed a fast exit. I immediately switched off the transmission. Clients didn't like having their conversations overheard.

To Dean, this club scene was just another day in the life of a professional football player, but to a girl who sat on the social-life sidelines, it was a bit overwhelming. He was my first celebrity client. Posing as a nanny, I'd protected children of billionaires, and as a sort of Girl Friday, I protected women leaders. Undercover work was my specialty. My diminutive size let me fade into the background. Pre-makeover, I would have stuck out like a sore thumb in this crowd.

Thanks to Joffrey's expertise, I wouldn't appear to be a fish out of water, even if I was swimming in doubt on the inside.

But I wasn't there to stargaze. Entering the club, I located the exits and noted where the bouncers were stationed. I made eye contact with two of Ian's Security's employees. Once I received nods of assurance, I relaxed.

Dean tried to position himself in front of me to bull his way through the crowd, but I couldn't let that happen.

"Alexa?" Jude Hastings, an ice hockey player with the Brooklyn Brawlers, blonde, blue-eyed, and built, greeted me with a hug.

I'd had a small crush on him in college. I should've melted into his embrace, except all I felt was Dean's body stiffening behind me. Jude pulled away, his hands lingering on my arms. He'd never looked at me like the way he was looking at me now.

"I almost didn't recognize you."

He shouldn't have recognized me at all. While I did tutor him in college, I'd done so wearing sweats, no makeup, and my hair swept up in a ponytail.

We made small talk for a minute until Dean cleared his throat and introduced himself. "Hi, I'm the boyfriend."

I bit my lip, realizing my social faux pas. But when was the last time I'd had to introduce anyone, never mind a boyfriend? "Oh, I'm sorry. Jude, this Dean Walker. Dean, this is Jude Hastings."

They shook hands. A little tug of war ensued between them. The two men were the same height, but as an enforcer in the NHL, Jude's body was more bulk muscular than Dean's quarterback lean and mean frame. Both of their smiles tightened as they jostled. Was this over me? How juvenile of them and, in all honesty, of me for being a little thrilled at the notion.

Some secret guy language passed between them, and the standoff ended.

"Well, it was good to see you, Alexa. Don't be a stranger." Jude winked at me, which I think was more for Dean's benefit than mine. *Men.*

"What was that he-man display for?" I took Dean's hand in mine and brushed my fingers over his palm. "Isn't this your throwing hand?" Reaching his wrist, I felt the beat of his pulse under the pad of my finger.

"Just playing my part."

His pulse jumped. I raised my gaze to see him swallowing a breath. Did my touch cause it? Impossible. "You could have an acting career once football is over."

Dean winced. "Never, ever talk about that. It's bad luck. Now I'm going to have to sacrifice a virgin to keep the football gods happy." His hot gaze swept me from toe to head. "You wouldn't happen to be a virgin?"

I snorted my reply. I'd had plenty of hookups over the years.

"With him?" Dean nodded to where Jude stood with a couple of beautiful women who were looking to score with the hockey star.

It hadn't been like that between us in college. I hadn't look like this back then. Hell, I hadn't looked like this last week. I was the little sister, the best buddy, the one you asked for help with homework. It hurt to admit that not Jude, or any of the student athletes, had paid attention to me, so I played it off. "No. I don't date jocks."

Dean turned his gaze back to me and then to my hand still holding his. "You're dating a jock now."

I dropped his hand like it was on fire, which explained the flames licking in my blood like a lit match set to a trail of gasoline. "Not really. This is a job. I was assigned to you."

"So this wasn't your idea?"

"Hardly. I'm used to being undercover, but never as someone's girlfriend."

Dean smiled, placing his hand on the small of my back, and whispered in my ear, "So in a way, I am your first."

Did that mean he planned to sacrifice me? A delicious chill skittered up from the base of spine where his thumb traced a circle.

"We should dance."

"No, we should not," I said, but Dean led me to the dance floor. "No, seriously." Dean twirled my body. "You do know that I'm armed, right?"

"Yeah, and dangerous," he said, pulling me into his arms.

My breath hitched, becoming shallow, as if I were dancing the salsa instead of swaying to the slow beat of some song I didn't recognize. The oxygen had been sucked out of the room, I was sure of it.

"You smell like candy apples."

And he smelled like spice and wickedness, while I'd never owned a bottle of perfume. "It's my conditioner."

"You feel good in my arms. Like you belong here."

"You can tone down the act."

"What if I told you it wasn't an act?"

By the bulge pressing against me, he didn't have to tell me, but maybe he should. Maybe I needed to hear it was all an act, because the fact that Dean had a hard-on for me was like a naughty fairy tale come true.

Another couple accidently bumped against us, jolting me out a lust-filled fog. Crap, I had forgotten why I was here. I looked to the left and then right for any possible threats. Other than a few curious stares, there was nothing out of place. I couldn't see behind him though, and that was a problem. With the other guards probably more interested in the hot women gyrating on the dance floor, I needed to stay hyper-vigilant.

I tried to maneuver my dance partner so I could get a better angle.

"Are you trying to lead?" The look on Dean's face

was a mixture of shock and amusement.

"No, well, a little. I can't see behind you."

Dean turned, his fingers threading through my hair to place his hand at the back of my head, and then he dipped me. "There, is that better?"

Oh, no, it was not better. Not. At. All. For one, it was hard to see upside down, and two, I'd rather be looking into his smoky brown eyes, and three, wetness slicked between my legs.

He whipped me back up, his hand drifting to the base of my skull. Our bodies pressed together, and we were no longer dancing. His shocked and amused expression was replaced by the intense fever in his eyes. His mouth was inches away from mine, our breaths mingling, charging the air around us. My heart fluttered as if a thousand bees were suddenly released from a cage inside my chest. Dean unlocked something deep inside me. Something I needed to slam shut before there was nothing left to protect.

The song ended, and I made an excuse to use the bathroom. I took a deep breath before alerting the team that I was on break.

"Some fancy moves out there, Reeves."

"Fuck off, Carter." Heat flamed my cheeks, but at least I knew the team had all eyes on Dean.

Opening the door to the well-appointed bathroom, I was besieged by the smell of hairspray and perfume. I took the opportunity to use the restroom since I never could be sure when I'd get another chance.

I washed my hands, taking a cursory glance in the mirror. A tall blonde bombshell sidled up next to me.

"You know you're gonna get hurt."

I arched a brow. "And you are…?" I told myself I was only asking as part of my job, and I was, despite the jealousy blindsiding me. The feeling didn't prevent me from noting how she'd said I'd get hurt, but failed to mention Dean doing the job.

"Just a friendly warning," she replied with a shrug.

I wasn't intimidated by her Amazonian height. She had no idea who she was messing with.

"I'd hate to see you get hurt," she repeated.

Hoping to get a rise out of her, I said. "Dean makes it hurt soooo good though, doesn't he?"

The mask of indifference transformed to an expression of hatred, worse than I'd seen on any mean girl in high school. Had I exposed Dean's stalker?

"Don't say I didn't warn you." Suspect number one twirled around and headed for the stalls.

Hayden Middleton, reality star and wife of the NY Cougars' quarterback said, "Don't mind her. You'll get used to the haters."

"Who is she?"

"She was a cheerleader for my Dad's team. I forgot her name. She probably blew someone to get in here."

"Why isn't she a cheerleader anymore?"

Hayden effortlessly swept the reddest of lipsticks across her second most famous body part. "She threatened another cheerleader."

"Sounds like a Lifetime movie."

"You have no idea. I'm Hayden."

"Ree—" Out of habit I almost said Reeves. "Uh, Alexa."

"So how long have you and Dean been dating?"

"Not long."

"By the way, I love your dress."

Did Hayden Middletown just say she loved my dress? Wait until I told Joffrey. Last week I was knee deep in kid duty, and now the queen of reality TV was admiring my outfit. Should I even be talking to the wife of Dean's enemy—the wife of my Fantasy Football pick? "Um, thanks."

"And I'd kill for your boots."

What would the ex-cheerleader sweeping by us and out of the bathroom kill for? *Fuck.*

"Thanks. I have to go. Sorry." I didn't have time for niceties and hoped Hayden wouldn't take offense at my abruptness.

"Blonde at your six."

"Well, that narrows it down. They're all blonde," said Carter.

"She's wearing a shimmering blue dress."

"Blue? Do you mean purple?"

Fuck! "Yes, purple." I cursed the partial color blindness that plagued me, keeping me from my childhood dream of being a police officer. Four years of straight A's and a criminal justice degree down the drain over a stupid test. I'd aced the NYPD physical fitness exam, beating most of the men, yet a condition that affected mostly men prevented me from wearing a badge. Now that was fucking irony.

"Got her. She's moving away from The King."

My co-workers thought the code name I'd given Dean was based on his football team, but to my secret shame it was inspired by his dic pic.

And now I'd left him alone in a crowded bar. Well, not alone. Ian's Security had personnel on the inside, but what if the so-not-a-cheerleader was the stalker? I'd dropped the ball. I had some nerve, accusing my male coworkers of endangering assignments.

As I weaved through the crowd, I was determined to squash any notions inside my head of Dean being anything other than a client, a body to be protected. It was a war of mind over matter.

"Purple Rain has left the building." Carter had already given our first suspect a code name.

Relief engulfed me as I approached the bar. Dean's charming smile made me wonder who would win the battle between my filthy mind and Dean's mighty-fine matter.

Chapter 7

Dean

ALEXA'S SMALL HAND was in mine as we waited for the valet to pull up with the SUV. The same hand that held a gun on me sent a tremor of desire through my body. It was hard to reconcile the two different sides of Miss Alexa Reeves. I could guess which one she preferred, and somehow I had to change her mind. This had stopped being a game to be won or lost.

The paparazzi got their fill of photos of me with my new fake girlfriend. Only it didn't feel fake, or rather I didn't want it to be.

The valet pulled up, and Alexa swooped in to snatch the keys, leaving me to handle the tip.

A reporter shouted out, "Too drunk to drive, Walker?"

Fuck. A headline like that was the last thing I needed. "Not at all." I pulled out a twenty and handed it to the valet. I turned back to the reporter before sliding in to the passenger seat. "You got something against women driving, buddy?"

"Good comeback, liar." Alexa smirked as I shut the door.

"What can I say? I'm a changed man," I half joked.

"Sure you are." She wasn't joking at all. Before driving off, she handed over her phone. "Do you know her?"

The face of a pretty blonde, but just the same as the next pretty blonde, stared back at me. "No. Why?"

"Are you sure?" She put the directional signal on and moved out into traffic. "Swipe to the next pic."

I did and took a closer look. The shot was taken outside the club, but I hadn't seen her inside. Then again, I'd been too focused on my tiny dancer to give much notice to any of the other women there. "I'm sure. Who took this?"

"One of the other guards."

"Why did they send it to you?"

She concentrated on the road, but it seemed like she was only trying to avoid answering. With the way she drove, she could talk and fend off an attacker at the same time. "Alexa?"

She took a deep breath and let it out with a whoosh. "She approached me in the bathroom, warned me that I was going to get hurt."

"What the fuck?" My mind reeled at the implications. By pretending to be my girlfriend had Alexa become the stalker's target? She'd walked out of the bathroom, cool as a cucumber, picking up right where we left off, flirting and driving me crazy with want. "I have no idea who she is."

"According to Hayden, she was a cheerleader with the Cougars."

"You met Hayden?"

"Really? That is what you're taking away from this conversation?"

I was such a dick, but if I was going to all this trouble to keep the threat a secret from my teammates, then I didn't want someone like Hayden to use it against the Kings. "No. No. It's just that... she knows you're my bodyguard?"

"Of course not." The edge in her voice relaxed as she continued, "We bonded over shoes and shit." She parked the SUV in the assigned spot in the garage and turned off the engine. Still looking ahead, she asked, "Have you dated any of the Kings' cheerleaders?"

"It's against the rules."

She turned to look at me. "I'll ask again. Have you dated any of them?" She put the word *dated* in air quotes. The light from the dash was still on, illuminating her delicate features.

"Off the record?"

"Unless one of them becomes a suspect, then yes, off the record."

Crap, I hated how this fun and potentially sex-filled

night had turned to absolute shit. "Molly and Bridget. But it was last season." Why was I acting so defensive about it? And why I was so concerned about the idea of her finding out that I did them together?

"Last names."

"Uh…" While I remembered each woman's face, I couldn't say I'd ever asked for last names. What was the point? Odd that I knew Alexa's last name before I even knew her first.

"Don't tax your brain. It's easy enough to find out," she said in a clipped professional tone.

I hated that tone. I liked her snarky and heated. Striding across the street, she was in full bodyguard mode, unlike when she was in my arms earlier. When I dipped her, I'd heard her breath catch in her throat. I almost kissed her before she ran off to the bathroom. She had been a woman in the midst of my seduction. There was no pretend between us. She wanted me. I wanted her. It should be simple, but like a typical woman, she made it complicated.

We rode the elevator in silence. She stared ahead while I couldn't keep my eyes off of her, hoping she'd looked my way. I missed the sexual tension sizzling between us but also, the camaraderie we built over the last few days. Thoughts of how I could bring back *that* Alexa rioted through my brain.

The elevator doors slid open, and she peeked out,

looking both ways before stepping out into the hallway. At the door to the apartment, she pulled out the gun hidden in her bra.

"Wait here," she ordered.

Not this time. I followed Alexa from room to room, ignoring her commands to fall back.

"I'm not your employee." If she thought I was going to stand idly by while she placed herself in harm's way because of me, then she thought wrong. I wanted to be there to push her out of the way or even jump in front of her if it came down to it. Would it even be a bullet? The letter hadn't elaborated on the means of my demise. A couple of days ago, I thought this was all a joke, but now I wasn't so sure.

She hesitated by my bedroom door.

"Is there something wrong?"

"No," she said, her voice tight with annoyance.

What was that all about? It went beyond being pissed at me for following her. Was she jealous of the cheerleaders? Was she mad that I was acting like this was a joke? But I couldn't let her know how affected I was at the thought of someone trying to hurt her.

She drew in a deep breath and let it go like she was trying to blow down the door like the wolf in the Three Little Pigs. Meanwhile, I was the real Big Bad Wolf, licking my chops laying in wait for her to enter my den.

She opened the door and headed for the bathroom. I

loosened the knot of my tie, yanked it off, and tossed it onto the unmade bed. Visions of tying a naked Alexa to the headboard crowded out all other thoughts.

Coming out of the master bathroom, she relaxed her stance and slid the gun into her bra holster. "Well, I'll leave you to... whatever." She looked calm, but her voice was full of apprehension.

Maybe now that she had done her job and we were safely in my apartment, she would loosen up a little.

I blocked her path, ready to run my Hail-Mary-pass play. I laid on the charm and smiled that smile that would make a nun leave the convent. "You didn't check under the bed."

"I'm sure there's nothing there but porn and a blow-up doll."

I laughed. "There's my Alexa."

"I'm not yours."

"Then you're a little too good at pretending to be my girlfriend."

"It's my job."

"No, you were enjoying yourself tonight. Why can't we mix business with pleasure? After all, what better way to keep an eye on me than to share my bed?"

"I'm held to a higher standard than you or my male coworkers."

How long was she going to hide behind that logic? "Spare me the feminist bullshit."

"It's not bullshit. You're a man. You don't understand."

"I understand you're scared of me."

She shook her head. "Am. Not."

"Yes, you are." I took a step closer. "Afraid of what I can do to your body." My fingers traced the curve of her cheek until I cupped her chin, tilting it so she had to look me in the eyes. "Afraid of the way I make you feel."

I saw her want, or maybe it was my desire reflecting back at me. The scent of caramel apples wafted in the air, reminding me of a long ago county fair I went to as a teen. I wanted to lick her. Take a bite out her. Knew once I got past the hard shell I'd taste sweetness and pie.

I bent my head, ready to meet the pink lips begging for mine. The breath between us heated and charged. I wanted her to come to me. The anticipation of her surrender was torture. I knew the reward would be heavenly relief. A little moan escaped her. The sound of it must have broken the trance she was under. She blinked and the hungry look was gone. I'd waited too long. *Fuck.*

"Wow, you are good." She placed a hand on my chest in a stopping motion. "In another life I might have fallen for it, but my job is a good enough reason for why I shouldn't cross that line."

With another woman I would've shrugged off the rejection, but beneath her hand my heart pounded for her, my blood racing to my groin. She'd made a mistake. Now she was more than a challenge—she'd made herself forbidden fruit. I told myself that was all this was.

A lie, but it was my lie to live.

"But I have big reason why you should." I hauled her up against my unmistakable hardness. The utter softness of her, melded to my body. To the world she wore an armor of toughness and indifference, but in my arms it all fell away.

Alexa's wicked smile signaled my victory. Then she whipped out her gun and pressed it against my cheek. "And I have a bigger reason why we shouldn't."

The cold steel against my skin was a relief compared to the heat she created inside me. "That is so fucking hot."

"You're a freak." Alexa pushed off my chest and backed off, now pointing the gun at the bulge in pants. "Let's see how freaky." Raising the gun, she motioned to my upper body. "Lose the suit jacket."

Holy crap! Where had this Alexa been hiding? Even in a dress that reminded me of cotton candy, she looked like a dominatrix ready to teach me a lesson. Did I want to be a bad or a good student? *Bad.* I wanted to be very, very bad. I was more than ready to get my freak on.

"Now."

Without hesitation I ripped the jacket off, forgetting the buttons.

"No," Alexa said sharply, as the ping of the buttons reverberated off the hardwood floors, one rolling under the dresser. "Do it slow." Her voice lowered to a sensuous hum. "Real slow."

Every article of clothing I wore constricted my body, like I was turning into the Incredible Hulk, and not because I was angry but because I was so fucking turned on. Because I needed to feel the cool air against my skin.

In an effort to calm my racing heart, I took a deep breath. Once composed, I undid the cufflinks, tossing them to bed next to the tie. Afraid she'd change her mind, I didn't dare move from my spot. The buttons holes of my shirt suddenly seemed too tiny—or if I was honest, my fingers too clumsy—to complete the task. I could thread a pass through three defenders to my receiver in the end zone, but right now my dexterity failed me. Finally, I was shrugging out of the shirt, taking my time even though I couldn't wait for my next command.

"Good. Now the belt."

I wasn't shy, holding her gaze as I unbuckled it, and then whipping it off, snapping the leather, taking gratification in her flinch.

"Don't give me any ideas," she said with a quick recovery.

The thought of her whipping my own ass with my belt held no appeal, so I put my hands on my hips and awaited her next move.

"Now the pants."

I undid the top button with a flick of my thumb.

"Unzip. Slow."

Like I had a choice. My cock was harder than it had ever been. I would risk injury to my most treasured body part if I didn't slide down the zipper with great care. My cock wasn't waiting for the next order, and I eased my ready-to-go erection out of my pants.

"Commando? You are such a slut."

"Been called a man-whore before but never a—"

"I didn't give you permission to speak."

Oh, holy hell. Was Alexa enjoying this as much I was? If so, there was no hint of it. Maybe she hadn't been kidding when she told my teammates she was a domina-trix.

"Drop 'em."

I gladly did as she asked, and then kicked my pants to land at her feet in a defiant gesture. She didn't yelled at me, probably because she was too busy staring at my dick.

"I will say this, the photo on your phone doesn't do you justice."

"Thanks." *I think.*

She motioned with her gun. "Now turn."

If she was trying to embarrass me, then she was going about it the wrong way. Being naked in locker room with a bunch of other naked guys and fully clothed coaches, equipment managers, and reporters coming and going was second nature to me. In front of a beautiful woman, naked was my natural state.

"You have a great ass. Spankable."

Looking over my shoulder, I said, "Thanks. I could use your vote on next year's FemaleFans.com 'Cutest Ass in the NFL' contest." I was used to being treated like a commodity on and off the field, but spankable took it to a raunchy level I wasn't sure I was comfortable with. My cock though was one hundred fucking percent on board. "Came in third."

"A travesty of justice to be sure." She quirked a smile. "Now shut up and turn."

Alexa bit her lip, looking a little unsure about her next move. Did she have the guts to take it all the way?

"Now what?" I asked, urging her on.

With an evil genius smile, she said, "Stroke yourself."

That was not what I had in mind. My cock ached, throbbing not for my touch but hers. For her mouth. For her pussy that I guaranteed was wet for me. "Alexa."

"Aww, is the game over already? How disappointing," she gloated.

Okay, so she had the guts to take it all the way. Did I? Hell, yeah. I grabbed my cock at the base. My hand glided over my thick six point eight inches in long, slow strokes. That's right I'd measured it.

"Good boy."

The lust in her eyes told me she wanted me just as much as I wanted her. This might have started as a game and she might have been on the offense, but I was winning now. Soon I'd have her writhing beneath me. Her pretty mouth would beg instead of barking orders. The thought of it rocked me, and my thighs quaked like a teenage boy.

"Lie on the bed."

Had she noticed the wobble in my legs? Stretching out on the mattress, I rested my head on the pillow, inclined perfectly so I could watch her. She stood at the footboard like some kind of angel dominatrix sent to take me on a trip through hell and heaven.

"Keep stroking. I want your cock harder than it's ever been."

It was so hard that it might break off. "Alexa, please. I'm going to come."

"Isn't that what you want?"

"With you. I want to come with you."

"Beg for it."

"I want you, Alexa." I'd done a lot of things, but I had never masturbated to a climax in front of a woman.

At some point she'd put the gun away. I could end this now. Grab her from where she stood and toss her onto the bed, but I wasn't sure how she would react. And honestly I didn't think I could stop our game without causing myself harm.

"Pump harder," she commanded.

"Alexa." My cock throbbed beneath my hand, and I could feel the come ready to erupt out of me. I'd never been so turned on, so hard, so everything in all my life.

"That's it. It's almost ready for me." Yet, she still had all her clothing on. Then Alexa slid the hem of dress up an enticing inch.

More. I wanted to see more. As if all the world's mysteries could be solved if I could see her panties. Then she made eye contact with me. Her gaze, wild and wanton. Why did she hold herself back?

"You're ready, Dean." She licked her lips like she was ready to taste me. Devour me.

I was undone. I came. Hard. I was fucking dying. Alexa was my executioner. And she didn't even need her gun.

Chapter 8

Alexa

H E WAS MAGNIFICENT. He was still an ass. But what an ass.

Dean Walker, the ultimate male specimen, coming at my command was an erotic sight to behold. I was a bad-ass vixen worthy of my own comic book series. Who was I kidding? If I was so bad-ass, I would've climbed in his bed and onto his beautiful cock. Instead I was no better than a voyeur watching on as he pleasured himself, his gaze full of want, blazing at me until he closed his eyes as his body shook and he shouted my name like a war cry.

To be honest, I'd shocked myself to my core, but as it wore off the recriminations began. I was a hypocrite of the worst kind. All those times I berated my male colleagues for sleeping with clients, and the first time I was tempted I'd surrendered to my base desires.

My mind reasoned with my conscience that I hadn't really crossed the line. I was in the clear. After all, my clothes were still on. I hadn't laid a finger on him, even though his body was created for hands-on exploration. In fact, I was a pillar of professionalism. Yeah, right. Dean had no shame and apparently neither did I.

Would Dean use this as an excuse to get me fired? Use it as blackmail to get me to do more?

Please, please use it as blackmail to get me to do more. No!

His body relaxed and his hand stilled. I headed for the master bath to get him a towel. Any excuse to escape the awkward moment that would ensue when he opened his eyes. Anything to get away from the mistake I'd just made.

I delayed my return, using the bathroom. I avoided looking in the mirror as I washed my hands. I didn't know what I would see. Regret? Desire? After enough dawdling, I walked back in. If I was lucky, he'd be asleep.

"There you are."

The smoky timbre of his voice created swirls of want inside me.

"For a second I thought I'd dreamed the whole thing." He patted the empty space beside him. "Come here."

Instead I threw the towel to his chest.

"Thanks. I think." He swept the towel across his body. "Alexa, talk to me."

The lights suddenly flickered, then darkness enveloped the room. Had the stalker saved me? Yep, I'd rather face off against a bad guy than talk to Dean about what just happened.

I grabbed my gun from the nightstand. "Wait here."

"Bullshit." He tossed the towel aside and swung his feet to the floor.

I didn't have time to argue with him. A sane man would have stayed hidden. Only a crazy one would go naked to a gunfight.

I couldn't control Dean, at least not without holding a gun on him, so I concentrated on what I could control. I itched to bypass the guest bathroom and workout room, but I was thorough and gave them a cursory scan before closing the doors. With my eyes adjusted to the darkness, I approached the living area. I could've sworn the drawn curtains were left open. Creeping closer, I realized they still were. All the lights in the city were out. A cloud drifted across the sky, revealing the moon. I heard Dean's footsteps behind me.

"Just a blackout," he said.

"I told you to wait," I hissed. Why was I disappointed to see he had put on pants?

"I'm not going to hide like a punk-ass bitch."

"So you're telling me if Oslo or Williams were here, you'd be in your bedroom right now?" He paused long enough for me to continue. "Thought so."

"I can protect myself."

"You have to let me do my job. You have to have

confidence in my ability to protect you."

"It has nothing to do with your abilities. At. All." He cut the air with his hand. "It has everything to do with me. You're not taking a bullet for me."

"It's my job. It's nothing personal."

"What?" Dean nodded and tilted his head in disbelief like he was channeling Robert De Niro. "How much more personal can it get?"

"It can. It just did. Or almost did." I was the one who'd dodged a bullet tonight.

"We can remedy that. Come back to bed." The moonbeams skimmed over his body, giving him the appearance of a man ready to morph into a werewolf.

"To be clear, I was never in your bed."

"Oh, going to play that card? The old 'oral isn't sex' argument."

Oral. Sex. My cheeks bloomed with heat. I turned away from him so the moonlight wouldn't reveal the gleam that had to be in my eyes. Thoughts of riding out the blackout on top of his cock rocked inside my mind. "We did not have... that."

"You know what I mean."

My phone buzzed. *Crap.* That had to be Dubois. I had forgotten to check in. I should hand in my resignation or at the very least ask to be reassigned. As I put down my gun on the coffee table, I decided to play dumb.

"What's up, Dubois?... A blackout?... I didn't know... I was sleeping... Yeah, I'll check on him now."

I swear I could feel Dean arch an eyebrow.

"Shut up. Go back to jerking off," I told Dubois and ended the call—and just in the nick of time.

Dean roared with laughter. I laughed too, realizing what I'd said.

An awkward silence followed. Finally, Dean said, "Well, goodnight."

"Dean?"

He turned around, his voice hopeful. "Yeah?"

"You're not going to tell anyone, are you?"

"I'm not the kiss-and-tell type of guy."

"Then I'm in trouble since we didn't actually kiss." How could I command him to do those naughty things in his bedroom and not even have gone to first base with him yet?

He stalked over to me. "Well then, you better shut me up and let me kiss you."

My mouth dropped open.

"I'll take that as a yes." His lips caressed mine. A little squeak escaped me, and I felt his smile upon my mouth. But he didn't stop.

I might have been able to fight a demanding kiss, but I had no safeguards in place for the slow and steady rush in my blood as his lips played along mine. This was a kiss of seduction. A kiss meant to change my mind. To change my whole world.

My body, always on the ready, released its tension and melded to him. The feel of his naked chest beneath my fingers made me want to dig my nails in like a feline creature and never let go. Dean touched his tongue to mine and I returned his kiss, mirroring his moves.

His hands drifted to my behind and gently squeezed.

The lights sputtered back on. Or maybe I had just realized it in that second. Our lips parted and my heart cracked open.

"Wow," he said, his eyes heavy-lidded from the slow burn of our kiss. "You pack a sweet punch, Alexa."

He let me go, and I stepped back. Though I was fully clothed, the chill of the dark void he left between us made me shiver.

"My door is always open," he added before disappearing down the hall.

Under the cover of darkness, I might have abandoned my last shred of dignity or any semblance of professionalism. With the lights on, my head had cleared and exposed me for what I was—*scared*. And it had nothing to do with losing my job at Ian's Security and everything to do with losing my heart to Dean.

PROTECTING A QUARTERBACK among eighty thousand fans was a bodyguard's nightmare. The stadium's security was one of the best in the nation, but they were looking for the threat to come from a terrorist, not a lone stalker. As Dean's girlfriend, I was stuck in the box seats set aside for family and friends. I had to trust in Oslo, Williams, and the rest of the security detail to keep Dean safe. Ian's Security believed in being proactive, and the team met once a day for updates and to go over and over different scenarios.

Approaching my seat, I noticed a long box stretched across the arms of the chair. Flowers? My body tensed and my senses heightened when I looked and saw no card.

"What did you do last night?" asked a wife or a girl-friend of one of Dean's teammates. I wasn't sure who was who yet.

Was this simply a mean girl trick? Unlikely. This wasn't high school. I couldn't let my old insecurities creep back in and affect my reasoning. Maybe, they were from Dean? Even more unlikely. That left only one alternative—his stalker. I felt paranoid, but no one ever got in trouble at Ian's Security for being too careful. Better paranoid than dead.

My earpiece was already on so I could hear my co-workers reports throughout the event. I turned my face away and explained what was going on. "What should I do?"

"Don't open it!" my boss screamed in my ear.

"No shit, Sherlock," I replied, shaking my head. I wasn't some rookie on her first assignment. At most jobs I'd be called on the carpet for the remark, but in the male-dominated world of security, it was expected.

"Meet me at the Billings' private elevator. There's a scanner at Gate B."

I gently picked up the box. The players' girlfriends and wives were looking at me expectantly. "Uh, I'm just going to put these in some water." I bit my lip and rolled my eyes to the heavens at my dumb excuse. Like where would I find a vase in a football stadium? Geez.

I carefully carried the box to the elevator, just in time for the doors to slide open. I went to step in.

"No. I'll take it," said my boss, relieving me of the box. The six-foot-five, former college football player and Green Beret had been in his glory inside the owner's box. I thought he'd be pissed about being called away for what could be nothing. But the gleam in his eyes told a different story. He'd been riding his desk too long and missed being in the thick of the action.

"But—"

"Go back to your seat like a good girlfriend."

Before I could argue, the doors slid closed. Fuming, I strode back to my seat. Dean had just taken the field.

In between downs, I made small talk with the two women closest to me while speculating on the others around us. None of them were like me. Yet another place where I didn't fit in. I was the shortest by far. My makeup was the bare minimum, while they had their faces painted on like they were competing at a beauty pageant. My shoes were practical, one-inch-heeled booties while some of the others sported stilettos in thirty-degree temperatures! They probably wondered what Dean saw in me.

Why hadn't Dean said something about my attire? As the quarterback's girlfriend, I was probably expected to dress to impress. But this was a football game for Christ's sake, not a dance club.

I slid the binoculars out of my bag and made a slow sweep of the stadium. My eyes landed on the Kings' cheerleaders. The security team had performed background checks, but other than some sex tapes, they all were clean. I continued my sweep as I wondered which ones Molly and Bridget were. If it wasn't important to the case, I didn't want to know. *Liar.*

"You don't seem too interested in watching your man play," said Kelly, the wife of one of the running backs.

"I can't stand to see Dean get hit," I lied. Or perhaps it wasn't a lie. He might not have been my Fantasy Football pick, but I didn't want him to get injured on or off the field. It was up to his lineman to protect him from the other team's defense.

"You'll never make it as a quarterback's girlfriend.

He's the other team's number one target."

Yep, Dean Walker was a walking bull's-eye.

"Reeves?" said Ian in my ear.

"Yeah." I got up and headed for the concession stand so I wouldn't draw any curious stares. They already thought I was a little off.

"Looks like you pissed off someone real good."

"They weren't flowers?" People buzzed around me, going and coming to and from, buying food or making trips to the bathroom.

"Oh, they were flowers. Dead ones. Dead roses to be exact."

My stomach fell. I spun around. Everyone looked like a threat, everyone looked innocent until they all became a sea of blurred faces.

"And there's something else."

Buck up, Alexa.

"Bring it," I said, determined to prove to Ian that I was as tough as any male in his employ, especially after that "like a good girlfriend" remark.

"There's powder residue on the tips. We have no choice but to involve the FBI. I'm sending it to their lab for testing. Probably just baby powder but…"

Ian didn't need to finish the sentence. I knew Dean wasn't the only walking bull's-eye in the stadium. Were the flowers from the girl I had the run-in with at Martini Madness? Or were they from some other jealous female, prompted by the photos in the gossip pages of Dean and I holding hands outside the club? The guys on the detail ribbed me endlessly about it. I was used to disappearing into the background not being thrown into the spotlight. Hopefully my new claim to fame would be yesterday's news by the time I moved on to my next assignment.

"You made the stalker make a move. Good job, Reeves."

Why did that praise suddenly seem hollow? And was I more upset that I'd become the stalker's target or that we were one step closer to catching her, thereby ending my pretend relationship with Dean?

Chapter 9

Dean

FOURTH AND GOAL.

Early in the game, conventional football strategy would tell you to kick a field goal and take the three points. My coach, God bless him, was a rebel. That's why we got along so well. With three failed attempts by the running backs to break the plane, the offensive coordinator radioed in a pass play to the tiny speaker in my helmet. After relaying the risky call to my teammates, we lined up.

I took the snap, dropped back, and scanned the field for my options. There were none. Like a charging bull, Dawson, the Steelheads defensive back, broke through the offensive line. *I'm fucked.*

I scrambled until I saw it, a glimpse of daylight. I ducked like a matador, Dawson missed me, and I headed for the gaping hole that opened up like the parting of the Red Sea. It collapsed just as quickly as I was pounded from both sides by the defensive tackles. As I was about to hit the ground, short of the paint, I felt the bulk of my three-hundred-pound center, Jacobs, pushing me from behind, punching my body past the goal line and into the end zone.

Touchdown!

Though underneath the crushing weight of a half a ton of bodies, I didn't feel a twinge of pain. I knew I'd feel every ache tomorrow. Right now only glory rushed through my veins as eighty thousand fans cheered. Jacobs hoisted me off the turf to inflict further damage to my person with a congratulatory shake and a clack of our helmets.

"You can run, but you can't hide," shouted Dawson as I jogged by.

"Look at the scoreboard, fuck-face." Somewhere down the line, maybe even today, I would pay dearly for that remark.

Coming back to the sideline, I was riding high. The celebration was quickly over as the offensive coordinator handed me the iPad so I could review the defense's positioning and go over the plan for the next possession.

Oslo and Williams flanked me. Something was definitely wrong. "What's going on?"

Oslo handed me a water bottle. "It's under control."

"What's under control?" I heard the panic in my voice and dialed it back a notch. "Is Alexa okay?"

Williams smacked me on the shoulder pad. "She's

fine, bro. Reeves is tougher than she looks."

Alexa talked a good game, but what did I really know about her abilities? She acted like she was ten-foot-two instead of five-foot-two. How was I supposed to play football when she could be in danger? Why was I only thinking of her when there was a stadium full of fans, concession workers, and players?

The crowd exploded. Panic clenched my gut, but it was just the fans' reaction to our defense intercepting the ball. I welcomed the opportunity to be back on the field where things made sense and the real world faded away.

After three failed downs, I trotted to the sideline to let our punter kick the ball, pissed that I'd failed to convert the turnover into points. I scanned the section where I knew the players' girlfriends usually sat. I'd never had a girl at a game. Not even my mom, who preferred to watch from home. After I realized watching me play reminded her too much of my father, I quit inviting her. I understood, because in way, having her here would do the same thing to me. I wondered what she would think of Alexa and mentally shook the crazy thought out my head. The women I brought to my apartment weren't the type you took home to meet mom.

At that exact moment I spotted her and relief engulfed me. Maybe now I could get my head back in the game where it belonged. With a win we could coast into the playoffs.

And that's exactly what we did.

For the most part the media loved me. I was the quotable quarterback, the one who talked trash, and I usually stuck around until all their questions were answered. Not today. Keeping the locker room interviews short and the press conference even shorter, I ducked out, anxious to find out what had happened and to see for myself that Alexa was okay.

She was smiling, chatting with some of my teammates' girlfriends in the VIP area. I guessed I'd worried for nothing. Yet, when I drew closer, I could see that her smile was a fake one.

"Dean! Great game." She walked over, mouthing, *Save me.*

From what though? From a conversation with a bunch of flighty women only concerned with fashion and money or...

"What the hell happened?" I asked in a tight whisper close to her ear.

"Nothing."

She was lying. But this wasn't the time or place for me to call her on it. I kissed her for the benefit of the others watching us. I continued the kiss for my enjoyment. Damn, she was sweet. Tasted of candy popcorn and surrender.

From faraway I heard one woman clear her throat. Then another said, "Geez, get a room."

Alexa broke the kiss and backed off, her cheeks tinged pink. The shy smile she wore now was real.

"Don't worry, they're just jealous," I whispered. "Let's go."

Alexa waved goodbye to the group.

"Aren't you coming out with us?" asked Jacob's wife.

After a win at home, a large group of them would go out for a celebration meal. I usually had better things to do. Now with a girlfriend I'd be expected to go.

Alexa turned back. "No, we're going to do as you suggested and get a room."

I hooted with laughter. Alexa was one of a kind. Ballsy and beautiful. If only she meant what she'd implied. Once in the cocoon of the car, I turned serious. "Okay, cut the shit. What happened?"

"Is that a nice way to speak to your girlfriend?"

How she enjoyed throwing my words back at me. She was too smart for her own good, but that's what I liked about her. And that was scarier than a charging linebacker.

"Alexa?"

"Fine." Like a sports announcer, she gave a play by play of the events that had unfolded while I was on the field, adding a little dig along the way. "I knew the flowers couldn't be from you, so I..." And so on.

All this time I was convinced the threatening letter was a joke. I'd only been humoring Alexa and my boss by allowing the security detail. Now though, without doubt, I realized someone wanted not only me but Alexa dead. What if it had been a bomb instead of dead flowers?

"There was some sort of white residue on the tips. It's being sent to the FBI for testing."

Alexa was in danger because of me. I wouldn't have it. If anything happened to her because of me, I'd be the biggest asshole on the planet. "You are fired. If you aren't my girlfriend, then you won't be a target."

"Dean, part of the point of me posing as your girlfriend is to transfer her focus from you to me."

"That's insane." *Who does that?*

"That's my job."

"Well, fuck your job." So much for me not cursing around women, but Alexa was beyond frustrating—besides she talked like a guy. And kissed like a siren determined to bring me to my knees and make me beg for more than kisses.

"Well, fuck you too," she said with all the charm of a sailor.

"Please do."

The corner of her mouth lifted into the beginnings of a smile. "In your dreams."

"Every night, baby doll."

Alexa stopped at a red light. "Easy, Superman."

I had a feeling she'd never let me forget greeting her at the door in my Superman boxers. We joked easily and naturally the rest of the way home. Alexa probably thought I'd dropped the issue of her remaining as my bodyguard, but first thing in the morning, I was calling my agent. Until then, I'd be the one doing the protecting.

Unlocking the door to my apartment, I used my body to block her from entering first.

"Dean, this is not funny."

"Damn straight it isn't." I opened the door, charging in to leave my bodyguard to close and lock it. Stomping my way through each room, I ignored Alexa's warnings that she was going to kill me first.

Conveniently, she ended up in my bedroom before me.

"You're an idiot." She placed her gun on the nightstand and fisted her hands on her hips in that "you are so in trouble" stance I'd come to adore. "What's wrong with you?"

I closed the distance between us and pulled her to me. "You. You are what's wrong with me," I growled. Then I unleashed my frustration upon her lips. Just as abruptly I broke away. I needed to know that she felt the same way. "I burn for you, Alexa."

Our panting breaths mingled until we are inhaling the same heated air.

"Dean, I can't—"

"*Can*, yes, you can."

"It's complicated."

"No, it's not. It's the most basic yet raw feeling in the world."

I felt her indecision. Felt the war between her body and mind. I knew her analytical brain would never surrender, so I stopped using words and appealed to her body, using my mouth in a more persuasive way. Placing kisses on her neck, nipping the lobe of her ear. With each silent plea of my mouth, she relented just a little more.

"Dean, this isn't fair."

"I happen to know you like to play dirty." I kissed her again so she couldn't say no, waiting until her mind caught up with her body that was saying, *Yes, yes, oh God, yes.* Alexa's wild response to my urgent touch was driving me insane. I caressed the curve of her hip, then up the side of her breast—

Wait, what was that?

"Is that a gun or are you just happy to see me?" I whipped off her sweater.

"I believe that's my line." She placed a firm hand on the outline of my hard cock pressing urgently against my zipper, handling him with the same confidence that she handled her gun. The she stepped back. "Safety first."

From the fabric holster of the bra, she drew out a small gun and then from the other side, slipped out an ammo magazine. God help the man who pissed her off. Perhaps, she *could* take care of herself.

I helped her struggle out of the bra. But anything worth having was worth fighting for, as the saying goes. Her breasts were perfect. They fit in my hands as if made from a mold of my cupped palms. With a moan, Alexa leaned into me, searching for more. The tilt of her delicate chin, the slight parting of her lips were a clear invitation to devour the taste of her. I accepted. I couldn't get enough of her sweetness and sass. I kissed her with a hunger that could never be sated.

She pushed off me and stripped off my shirt.

"Any more weapons I should know about?"

"Wouldn't you rather frisk me and find out for yourself?"

I answered by dropping to my aching knees to run my hands along her legs. Sure enough I felt a slight bulge on her right thigh. A knife? Another gun? Oh man, what a fucking turn on. I thought my type was a bubblehead blonde when all long it was a bewitching brunette packing heat. "What do we have here?"

She smiled down at me and unbuttoned her pants, but I was impatient and helped with the rest of the task of shedding them. Practical panties aside, the plain garter she wore was still sexy, perhaps even more so because of its purpose. I slid a sinister looking dagger out of the casing. A normal man would have second thoughts. But I obviously wasn't normal by any standards.

"You won't be needing this," I said, tossing it toward

the closet.

She put a finger underneath my chin, lifting it so I would look her in the eyes. Then she stroked my cheek like I was her pet. "As long as you please me, I won't."

I should be running for the door with my cock tucked between my legs, but this woman fascinated me, as if she held some sort of ancient power over me. Or was it simply because she didn't take my bullshit. Called me on it. Turned it around on me so I was the one doing the begging? Clearly, since I was the one on my knees.

Leaving her garter on, I yanked off her undies. Groomed but not shaven. I wondered what secrets she still kept from me. "Are you hiding anything else, baby doll?"

"Perhaps your tongue should give me a thorough inspection."

I couldn't remember the last time I'd been so turned on. I knew for certain I'd never been so entertained by foreplay. I pressed my mouth against the vee at her thighs. Using my hand, I pulled her thighs apart and licked. Nothing nefarious awaited me here. Only a sweet nirvana. I licked and sucked. She grabbed my shoulders, digging her nails into my flesh. *Oh, yeah, that's going to leave a mark.* Battle wounds I'd gladly take to the grave.

"You are very thorough," she said in a breathless moan.

"You ain't seen nothing yet." I picked her up as I

stood and threw her onto the bed in one fluid motion.

She giggled, but she didn't laugh for long. Pulling her thighs roughly to me, I settled my head between her legs and gave the word *thorough* a whole new meaning. Savoring each moan, each yank of my hair, each push of her pussy into my mouth, I was driven to madness with the taste of her. I wanted to tease her with my tongue, but I needed her orgasm as much as she did. Needed to know I could melt the steely armor of the woman who challenged me like no other. Her thighs began to tremble. The bud of her sex tightened. I could feel her release ready to rock. Alexa cried for mercy. Cried for God, then shouted my name as she let go and became mine.

I raised myself up on my forearms and watched her writhe beneath me, still floating down from the highest of highs. *I did that.*

"I'll return the favor later. Right now, I need you inside me." Her voice—velvety from lust, yet husky from shouting my name—had lost its hard edge.

"Believe me, it was no favor and all my pleasure." I was so fucking turned on by the way she pushed me onto my back and relieved me of my pants in record time. I grabbed a condom from the nightstand and rolled it on.

Alexa straddled me. Her liquid heat dripped onto to my balls, and I jerked in reaction.

Her lazy smile, messy hair, and drowning eyes were all the thanks I needed. Then she slid down my shaft and

I amended that statement to include her hot, wet pussy on top on me. Damn, she was tight. Rocking her hips, she pressed her lips together, like she was trying to hold herself back from me. From herself. I was having none of it. Here, in my bed, there would be nothing between us. I wanted everything she had to give.

"Take me for a ride, Alexa."

The lazy smile was back, and I felt like the world belonged to me. She pressed a hand to my chest and rode the full length of me. At a nice easy pace, I memorized each move, learning the way she liked to be touched. Her breasts bounced enticingly close to my mouth, but not close enough. Then she straightened, tossing her head back, her hair falling around her shoulders in a wild mane as she rode me hard and fast.

"That's it, Alexa. Break me."

It might have been better if she had. Alexa was feral, yet tamed me with each lift of her hips. She was free, yet owned all of me with each downward stroke of her pussy. In the moments between heartbeats, I was held captive. And I had no escape plan.

Chapter 10

Alexa

I DIDN'T CARE that I'd risked everything. I'd gained something more precious than any job.

And I wasn't talking about Dean. God knew, the man creating the delicious thrum through my whole being wasn't mine. I had absolutely no delusions on that. He wanted me off his detail. If he pressed hard enough, he'd get his way. Why not enjoy one night of abandon? Either way, I was screwed. It might as well as be the enjoyable kind.

Enjoyable was the understatement of all time. Dean delivered on all the promises his body made. I still hummed with the release from his mouth on my pussy, and now his hard cock stoked a fire deep within me. I feared I would burn from the intensity building with each thrust of my body down onto his. I was desperate, beyond caring what would happen in the aftermath. A sexual feminine power rose up within me.

I wanted. I needed. I desired. Was desired.

By him.

Dean gripped my hips, holding me steady while I rode him. He urged me on. Told me to use and abuse him. And I did. My nails dug into his ripped abs. A slick sweat broke over our bodies.

"Alexa, I can feel you."

I could feel him too. Feel his whole body tighten, ready for release. We were synced as one. I let go and came. Waves and waves of pleasure doused the fire raging in my blood. My name tore from his mouth and his from mine until only our panting breaths filled the silence.

I collapsed on top of him in a heap of exhausted liberation. But just as quickly I lost my heart to Dean when he wrapped me in the warmth of his embrace. He held me like he was never going to let me go. I hoped he never did.

TURNED OUT, I was as bad of an influence on him as he was on me, except I tempted him with food. Instead of having one of his prepared healthy barf meals, Dean dove into the Chinese food I had delivered. Like a scene out of a chick flick, we sat on the bed cross-legged with the lights dimmed low. Cartons of fried rice, lo mein, moo shu pork, and boneless spareribs sat on a tray between us. Famished from our sexual play, we both ate like we hadn't had food in days. I hoped we were refueling for another around.

His white t-shirt swam on me, and he had slipped on his Superman boxers, which I found out were a gift from his nephew. I wondered if he planned to be a father someday, and I was horrified when the thought flew out of my mouth. "Do you want kids?"

"Are you offering up your womb?"

"I believe I already did." I started stuffing my face to shut myself up.

"Someday. How about you?"

"Are you offering up your sperm?" I asked with my mouth full. *Real attractive, Alexa.* His sperm were swimming backward as we spoke.

He laughed. "I believe I already did."

"No, you didn't. It's inside the condom, in the trash can."

Dean nearly choked on his food. "Always have to have the last word, don't you?"

I shrugged, stuffing in another mouthful of lo mein.

Dean put down his chopsticks on the tray. "Man, that was so good. I don't know why, but I actually feel better after eating this than those meals."

"Yeah, all that healthy eating will kill you. It makes your immune system lazy."

"Love your twisted logic. But you'll crash sooner or later from all the crap you eat."

"Not to be dramatic or anything, but when you have a job where there's a possibility of getting killed, you don't give much thought to the food you're eating."

"Why do you put your life on the line for someone you don't know?"

Crap, I shouldn't have brought that up. Was it too much to hope that my skills in the bedroom would make him forget my duties outside of it? Or was this seduction just his pleasurable way of getting me fired? If so, then I'd read him wrong. If I didn't know any better, I'd say he was trying to get to know me, or maybe even to understand me.

I was going to shrug the question off, but if he knew how important this job was to me, he might not pull the trigger to get me fired. "I was going to be a cop, like my whole family."

"A family of cops? That explains a lot."

"What's that supposed to mean?" If he dared to mention my makeover, I was prepared to repurpose the chopsticks as a stake and ram them through his heart.

"You're ballsy. Nothing seems to affect you."

That last part wasn't true. Some days it seemed liked everything hit me square in the chest, but in my family and with most cops that I knew, we tamped down messy feelings until they were buried six feet under. Buck up and suck it up.

"And then there's the way you handle your gun...

and mine."

My heart flipped at his sexy grin and mischievous gaze. Or maybe it was the Chinese food causing indigestion, and I was one burp away from being cured. My belching abilities went a long way with my coworkers, but I wasn't about to do it in front of Dean. The snort laugh that was my MO was bad enough. "You like the way I handle your gun, uh?"

"Oh yeah. So why aren't you a cop?"

Bitter emotions roiled inside me at the unfairness of it all. "After I graduated with a degree in criminal justice, I took the NYPD exam."

"You failed it."

"Noooo." I poked him in the ribs with a chopstick. "I aced it, and I aced the physical fitness test too. Well, not aced, but I performed better than eighty percent of the males." How I loved to throw that statistic around.

"I'm impressed, but not surprised."

"Ha! You just assumed I'd failed."

"I know you're physically fit, obviously from the sex marathon we just ran, but I have to question the intelligence of someone who chooses your line of work."

"It chose me after I failed the medical exam. I failed the colorblind test. Apparently, I can't distinguish between certain colors. One of the instructors passed my name along to Ian, who's always on the lookout for recruits.

"But you'd still rather be a cop?"

I shrugged, even though yes, I'd give anything to be a cop. "Hey, at least I still get to carry a gun," I joked.

Dean wasn't fooled. He gently took my hand, rubbing his thumb along my palm. "You would have made a great cop."

His light touch, his caring gaze, and the low tone of his voice conveyed the sincerity of his words. In Billings' office he'd come across as an arrogant jerk, but underneath all the hype, Dean was actually a kind person. No, it was more than that. He was a loving person. Loving. *Love.* I bit my lip, but held his gaze unable to look away, mesmerized and drunk on his whiskey-brown eyes.

A moment passed between us. It scared the ever-loving shit out of me. Apparently it scared Dean too.

He released my hand and leaned forward to pick up the chopsticks. "You know you can arrest me anytime. Just bring the handcuffs."

"One day you'll regret that." I took another bite of lo mein, relieved that we were back to kidding around. If only my heart would return to its normal beat. And that had absolutely nothing to do with the Chinese food.

Chapter 11

Alexa

TWO WEEKS LATER, and Dean still hadn't tried to get me fired. My skills in the bedroom seemed to trump his concerns for my safety.

Or more likely, it was because the day after our sex marathon, we learned the residue on the flowers had tested positive for harmless baby powder. As far as Dean knew, I wasn't in danger.

What Dean didn't know was that the Kings' front office had received another threatening letter. I hoped to be long gone before he found out that Billings and his agent had decided to keep him out of the loop. While their reasoning had more to do with keeping the star quarterback's head in the game, mine had to do with staying on the job. I felt guilty, but I was Dean's best hope of staying alive. Besides, I wasn't ready to give up my role as pretend girlfriend, and if Dean realized the seriousness of the threat, I'd be his pretend *ex*-girlfriend.

Unlike some other security agencies that only reacted, Ian's Security was a diligently proactive firm. I took different routes to practice, left at different times, scrutinized his schedule, and the security team was sent ahead to recon anywhere Dean traveled.

During the season Dean ran an after-school program on Mondays at the Uniondale Middle School. The past couple of Mondays though, he'd been forced to cancel since it would be impossible to secure the site. Dean refused to disappoint the kids again, so he twisted Billings' arm, and the owner agreed to change the venue to the Kings' practice facility and even provided the bus to drive over the kids after school.

Dean and I were waiting on the short field inside the facility, which also housed an impressive weight room, a theater to watch game film, hot tubs, and other state-of-the-art training equipment.

Impressive as that all was, only memories of the horrors of middle school flooded my mind. I nervously bounced from toe to toe on the artificial turf. Joffrey had sent over some fashionable fitness wear. At first I scoffed at the clothes. Normally I worked out in a pair of baggy sweats and a raggedy t-shirt. No more. I was a convert. The body-hugging outfit with color blocks of black and white made me feel fierce despite my trepidation at facing a bunch of preteens. *I got this.*

"Why is it called Get Off the Couch?" I asked. For a moment it looked like he wasn't going to answer.

"I was a chubby kid. I played video games, and my best friends were a supersized soda and a bag of chips," he confessed.

I couldn't picture the ideal male specimen standing beside me ever having an ounce of fat on him or that a man who had tons of fans, at one time had no friends. In that last way we were more alike than I'd thought, except that at least I'd had Joffrey. "When did you decide to get off the couch?"

"I was thirteen."

"For a girl?"

Dean laughed. "Of course. Teenage boys will never change."

"Grown-up ones too."

"That's because we never grow up, baby doll." He tugged on my ponytail. "See? I've been itching to do that since this morning."

My face heated like a schoolgirl, but the desire coursing through my body was that of a woman. I wasn't even mad that he called me baby doll. In fact, I was growing to like the endearment. It was all the more reason to catch the psycho after him.

Without warning, about fifty boys and girls burst onto the field, whooping and screaming like they'd won the lottery. They gathered around us, trying to get Dean's attention all at the same time.

Dean blew the whistle. "Okay, guys." When they

quieted, he said, "Alexa here will be joining us today."

"Is she your girlfriend?"

"Uh, yeah."

Gee, such enthusiasm about admitting that. I chalked it up to Dean not wanting to lie to his students.

"Is she why we haven't seen you?" asked a boy with a scowl.

Great, they hated me.

"Not at all," Dean said.

"Are you going to get married?" asked one of the preteen girls.

"Wow." He scratched his head. "Well, uh…"

"He should be so lucky," I said, saving him from further questioning.

A few of his teammates eagerly joined us for tag football, and they all broke out into teams. I was declared the referee. There was one girl who didn't join in. I waved her over, but she sat rooted to her spot on the sideline.

Her classmates, though, were having a great time, yelling, tumbling, and laughing. They all adored Dean. Somehow he made them all feel special. Here on the field, Dean's surface persona of a rich, spoiled athlete changed and became something deeper. He cared about something other than himself. He'd tried to hide it earlier, but I suspected Dean had been taunted for being overweight.

As I grew to know the real Dean, my puzzlement about why someone would want to kill him had grown. It had to be a spurned lover. With my own feelings running amok, I could see how a female could become unhinged over losing him. But all of the exes had checked out.

I blew the whistle, calling a penalty on Dean for un-sportsmanlike conduct after he goosed his teammate Jacobs, who in this game was playing against him.

"What? But I'm your boyfriend!" he joked.

"Call 'em like I see 'em."

He picked me up and tossed me over his shoulder. "Water break," yelled Dean. The kids ran over to the sideline as he put me down. "Some of them are taller than you"

"Though she be but little, she is fierce."

"That you are. And smoking fine. I think all the boys have a crush on you."

About fifteen years too late. Not that I believed it.

I nodded toward the girl on the bench. "Why isn't she playing?"

"That's Tammy. My charms don't work on her. Be-lieve me I've tried."

"I'll go over and see what's up."

"Good luck with that."

Even sitting, I could tell Tammy was as tall as I was short. She had spiky, short blonde hair and a pair of stunning sky-blue eyes underneath enough goth makeup to make Joffrey breakout in hives. Where I'd tried to go unnoticed in school, she had decided to standout.

"Hi, Tammy."

Silence. Did I forget to the mention the invisible *fuck off* sign on her forehead?

What was I thinking? If Mr. Personality couldn't sway a preteen girl, how was a girl who sat on the sidelines the first twenty years of her life going to do any better? "Why aren't you having fun with the rest of us?"

"This is sooooo lame."

Oh, the attitude! But I recognized the defense mechanism all too well. "Then why are you here?"

"My mom made me."

I sat next to her. "You remind me of myself when I was your age."

"But you're pretty and girly."

Pretty? Oh, the makeover, I thought. But I wasn't dressed to impress and wore the bare minimum of makeup. "Thank you, but no more than you are."

She rolled her eyes at me. "Oh yeah, that's why you're going out with Dean Walker and all the boys pick on me."

My gut twisted with outrage, and my hands fisted in fury. I suddenly wanted to be thirteen again and have her point out every single boy who bothered her and pummel him to the ground. I drew in a deep breath to calm myself. My lingering anger would serve no purpose.

"I was bullied too, so was my best friend."

"No way. What did you do?"

Hmm… This was dicey territory. I wasn't qualified to give advice to a student. "Have you told a teacher?"

"It only got worse when someone else took over."

Should I tell her to stick up for herself? But what if she got hurt or got into trouble or turned violent?

It took several fights before my own tormentors decided I wasn't worth a broken nose. I almost smiled at the memory of sending Derek to the emergency room.

"Do you want me to say something? To the principal?"

Tammy vehemently shook her head no, but the blonde spikes remained structurally intact.

I patted her hand. "It gets better." *Now that was lame.*

Should I tell her that the pain of rejection might dull, but it remained a part of your psyche forever? That the doubt you thought buried six feet under could rise from the dead, making you question everything. That until less than a month ago, I was still that awkward girl on the outside?

Would this Alexa go back to being Reeves after the assignment was over? Could I?

"In the meantime," I said as I stood, "let me show you a few self-defense moves."

This time she answered with a wary nod.

On the sidelines I taught her to block punches, to deliver a kick to the shins, then up higher. Even that didn't produce a giggle out of her. Once she nailed those, I showed her, God forgive me, the eye gouge.

She was a quick and eager student. Twenty minutes later, Dean jogged over. "That's awesome," he said as he high-fived Tammy.

An ear-to-ear grin splashed across her face. I detected a blush as well. I couldn't blame her. I was pretty sure I had the same look on my face.

"Maybe next time you'll play?" Dean asked.

"Will you be here again, Alexa?" Her hopeful eyes tugged on my heartstrings.

"I guarantee it," Dean said.

I cringed at his promise. If I caught the stalker before next week, I'd be moving on to my next assignment. I could take an overdue vacation, but that would only delay the inevitable. It wasn't like Dean had confessed his undying love for me.

Outside of the bedroom, we kept things light and chill. Behind closed doors… or on the dining room table… or in the shower… or up against that closed door, we were heavy and hot with no promises spoken. And here he was offering a guarantee that I'd be around next week, when the only guarantee I could offer was that I'd never forget him.

Chapter 12

Dean

I WAS A genius. Alexa had reached Tammy when I couldn't, and I'd used that to put Alexa on the spot to ensure her continued participation in my after-school program. Now I had an excuse to see her when her job with me was over.

To think I originally wanted her off my detail, and now the only thing I wanted was more time to figure out how I felt about her. About us. *Whoa, take one giant leap away from that thought.*

So much safer to focus on how hot she looked in those body-hugging leggings. I could barely keep my concentration on the kids' game. My teammates had the same problem, which is why I goosed Jacobs after he eyeballed Alexa's ass longer than was respectful. She had no idea of her effect on men. On me. To add insult to injury, my little referee threw a flag on the play.

I ended the session with a stretching routine and then high-fived the kids as they left. Tammy was the last one in line. "Thank you, Mr. Walker."

"You're welcome, and it's Dean." Not for the first time, I wondered how Tammy's spiked hair stayed upright.

Before she left, she ran back to hug Alexa, who went wide-eyed with shock, but then returned the hug. "See you next week," Tammy said. She waved goodbye and followed her classmates.

Alexa turned toward me. "You shouldn't have promised I'd be here."

Crap, I didn't think she'd call me on that. I shrugged. "It's not like you're any closer to catching my supposed stalker." I flicked the football over to her.

"Touché." She caught it and tossed it back and forth between her hands. "Have you thought about adding in an anti-bullying program?"

"Why?"

"Because you need one. Tammy is being picked on."

I shook my head in disbelief. "They all seem like such nice kids." One of them had me completely fooled. "Who?"

"Tammy wouldn't say, which is probably a good thing. I'm sure the last thing you need is your hired gun giving one of those kids a wedgie and a black eye.

That Alexa had to fight off bullies as a child gnawed at my gut. That her insides were still obviously damaged left me at a loss of how to comfort her. To make it better. Honoring her request was the only way I knew to ease her mind. "Thanks for telling me. I'll look into it. Maybe even get some of the guys to help."

"Great, thanks!"

Her smile did things to my heart. Sometimes it was a flip-flop, other times a blow, or a simple skipped beat. Alexa was a pretty woman, but her real beauty glowed from the inside out.

Now I knew what her friend Joffrey meant about having Alexa as a protector. A fierce defender of the bullied and now mama bear to one of my after-school kids, she'd make a great mom. She said she wanted children—eventually. Somewhere deep inside I wanted that eventually to be with me. As long as that terrifying thought stayed buried, I'd be safe.

"What are you thinking?" she asked with an expression like I'd grown two heads.

Since I couldn't exactly admit to where my thoughts had led me, I said, "The self-defense moves you taught Tammy. Is there anything you can't do?"

"Yeah, knit you a sweater." She laughed and snorted.

The sound of it should have been a turnoff, but coming from her it was fucking adorable. I loved the way she scrunched up her tiny nose and the way her cheeks blushed when she realized the sound came from her. And I loved how she laughed at her own jokes. Loved even more when she laughed at mine.

"I said that to you weeks ago." I was surprised she remembered. That day in Billings's office seemed like a distant memory, so did the woman I'd met that day. Alexa was either a really good actress or she'd morphed into a one hell of a sexy woman right before my eyes.

"Oh, Dean, you should know that women never forget anything."

I did know, but increasingly I was beginning to forget things around Alexa. Mainly, that she really wasn't my girlfriend. Not officially anyway. Even before the nights of wild sex, it had been easy to slip into the role of boyfriend. And now it was all too real.

It wasn't like Alexa had asked for any promises. But she didn't seem the type to apply pressure for a commitment. Somehow I'd turned into the female in this relationship. Wondering where I stood, kids, promises of the future. And complaining when she left the bed at night to take vigil on the couch, when all I wanted to do was sleep with my arms wrapped around her. Letting her take the lead in the bedroom. Not that I minded. At. All. Alexa was sexy when she was bossy, but I was turning into a wuss and getting lazy. It was time to take the control back.

AFTER CHECKING THE apartment, Alexa stripped off her shirt in the living room. "I'm hitting the showers."

I followed her, but when she made the move for the guest bathroom, I steered her toward my bedroom.

"Dean, I'm all sweaty."

"Not what I had in mind, baby doll." I bypassed the bed for the bathroom. "Yet."

"What are we doing then?"

Reaching into the large tiled shower, I turned on the water. "Doing my part to save the earth." I tugged my shirt over my head.

"You have two showerheads and like eight water jets," she volleyed back, but she shed the rest of her clothes just as fast as I did.

"That's because I'm a very dirty boy."

"Then let's get you cleaned up." Alexa smacked my ass as I entered the shower ahead of her. She took a tentative step in. "It's too cold."

I adjusted the temperature. "Better?"

"No."

"Seriously?" I pulled her into my arms and she shivered. "Wow, you are cold. I'll warm you up." I kissed her under the hot spray. Steam rose around us, but I wasn't sure if the mist was from the water or if it was coming off of me.

"Better?"

"Much." She smiled.

Using the bar of soap, I lathered her body, memorizing every dip, every curve as my hands roamed freely.

"Your turn," she said, holding her hand out for the soap.

I shook my head. "We are saving the earth here, remember?" I rubbed my body against hers, sharing the suds between us.

She giggled. "You're crazy." We stood under the spray to rinse off. She looked up at me. "That was fun."

A charged moment hung between us. The feel of the water rushing around us, the sound of a thousand tiny droplets, the touch of our slick bodies, and the scent of my masculine soap captured an intimacy that I've never had with a woman.

Before I could make my move, Alexa turned off the shower. "Playtime is over."

Assuming her abruptness had something to do with being available to the security team, I grabbed a heated towel from the bar and patted Alexa's face, then her neck, then—

"I can dry myself off," she barked like I'd committed a criminal offense.

That was it. I tossed the towel to the floor. She was beyond frustrating. Couldn't she see I was trying to be romantic? I picked her up and took her to my bed.

"Dean!"

With both of us sopping wet, I threw her onto the mattress, and before she could protest, I pounced on her. She wiggled beneath me, wanting me to take her fast and hard.

"Not this time, baby doll." I kissed her soft and slow. She bucked, wanting more, always wanting more. She'd get it, but in my own sweet time.

Kissing her was like drinking apple bourbon. Smooth and sweet going down, packing a punch as it hit me in the gut, then the slow burn firing my blood. All from just kissing her. Drunk, I left her lips to trail little licks on her neck and down to her breasts.

I blew a breath over her nipple, and when it puckered, I fastened my mouth on it and sucked gently while rolling my tongue. Her breathy moans filled the room until I thought she would come. She pleaded for me stop, and then to never stop, erotic music to my ears.

My lips seared a path down to the flat plane of her tummy, my hands holding her hips so she couldn't squirm even as she tried to push my head down. God, she was strong. I whipped my head away.

"Dean, don't tease me."

From the apex of her thighs, I looked up. "I'm not trying to tease you, Alexa. I'm pleasuring you.

"This is torture," she mumbled, "Against the Geneva Convention."

I chuckled. Easing her ache, I licked her pussy until it was swollen and rosy. I slid in two fingers, gently massaging while I continued to toy with the nub of her sex with my tongue.

"Dean. Stop. I can't..." She sucked in a breath. "Take it."

"Trust me, Alexa," I said, my voice hoarse and low.

I went back to work with my tongue, hooking my fingers inside her. Her body lifted off the mattress as she tensed, and her breath hitched as she struggled for air until I thought I might have to revive her with a little mouth to mouth. Then she let go. Sobbing my name like I'd left her instead of staying the course and finishing her off in glorious waves.

My hand moved over her shaking body, soothing her. "Alexa, you are so delicious. So beautiful."

"Don't ever do that again," she said, her chest still heaving for air.

"What?" I asked, confused, stunned by her reaction. "Give you a rocking orgasm?"

"No. Make me want more."

Still confused, I asked, "More orgasms?"

A brief sadness shifted over her face, then annoyance. "Of course, orgasms."

I smiled, but in a way I was hoping for a different answer. I should've been relieved she was cool with the status quo. Instead I was the one who was left wanting something I couldn't express. "Babe, that's not a problem."

I grabbed a condom from the nightstand and tossed it to her.

"Roll it on."

Alexa hated taking orders, which made it all the more gratifying when she relented and obeyed. I nudged her back to the mattress when she was done. In the dim light I could see the annoyance was gone, her misty blue eyes only shining with desire. I flinched as she raked her nails down my abs.

"Dean, patience is not one of my virtues."

"Ah, but it is one of mine." I grabbed her wrists together with one hand and pulled them above her head. Her blue eyes widened, but she didn't put up a fight as I slid into her hot, wet heat, welcoming me home.

Home.

This wasn't about getting off. It wasn't even about the sex. Instead of release I wanted a connection with Alexa beyond the raw need of our bodies joining. I craved a mind-to-mind union, a heart-to-heart bonding. Man, I hadn't turned into a wuss at all. It was so much worse than that.

I'd fallen in love.

Chapter 13

Alexa

I TRIED TO resist the slow burn smoldering in my blood. Tried to turn myself cold to it. But Dean melted the icy depths within me. Shined a light in the dark corners of my psyche. The cool and collected Reeves was nowhere to be found.

My body craved hard and fast, but in the deep recesses of my heart, in my soul, I yearned for this. Needed his deep, desperate thrusts. Delusional from his kisses, I pretended Dean's body was telling me without words how he felt. And it felt like love.

This was dangerous. He was dangerous.

"This is real, Alexa."

What was real? Us? Then he was just as foolish as I was. We could never work. Our relationship was a mirage. The hot fusion of our bodies was merely a result of us being thrown together in close confines without any outlet but each other.

"Fuck me, Dean." I begged for him to go full throttle. The raw sex I could handle—the raw emotions flooding in overwhelmed me. Tears pricked my eyes.

"No, Alexa, this feels too good, too right." His voice came out in a strangled whisper, like he was struggling to keep the pace passionate and meaningful.

Hanging on for dear life, I dug my nails into the muscular cords of Dean's shoulders.

"That's it, Alexa. Mark me." His teeth grazed my neck.

The slow burn surged into a raging firestorm. I teetered on the brink of madness. And then I fell. Which side I would come out on was unclear as pleasure tore through my entire being.

"Stay," he murmured against my ear as he rolled us over.

Instead of panic at his soft plea, I settled into his embrace like a satisfied kitten. I might have even purred.

OVER THE NEXT few weeks, Dean chalked up his ongoing stomach problems to nerves. From worry over making the playoffs to actually making them, he was a mess. He scoffed when I suggested he was worried about the death threat or that something could be medically wrong. *Men.*

The playoff game to decide who would go to the Super Bowl was about to start. After vomiting most of the night, Dean had looked pale and drawn this morning. I drove him to the stadium early so the team doctors could evaluate him. Since as a mere girlfriend, I was banned from the locker room, I had Oslo radio updates on Dean's condition. With an IV administered to replace fluids, it would be a game-time decision if he played. But I knew Dean inside and out. They'd have to sedate him to keep him off the field.

Since the team hadn't taken the field yet, I was indulging in a stadium bratwurst roll with the works.

"Hey, Reeves," Ian called from behind me.

The sound of my last name took a moment to register in my brain. Funny how in just a few short months, I'd grown to prefer Alexa to Reeves.

I turned. "Yeah, boss?"

"I just talked to Walker. He's going to play. By the way, he says you're annoyingly professional."

"That's me." Why had Dean gone out of his way to lie for me?

"I thought you should know that Billings is pulling the plug on Walker's detail when the season's over."

"But what if we haven't caught the person who wrote those letters?" The owner's pretty speech about protecting his players was bullshit. His only concern was a championship. Yet, it was Dean's only concern too, foolishly risking his health by playing today. *Men.*

"I'm sure Walker can afford his own security, though

I doubt he'll continue since he didn't want you in the first place."

As if I needed a reminder. "Well, maybe if we were honest about the recent rash of letters, he might take this more seriously."

"Reeves, we've been through this. And you've done a great job. I was going to wait to tell you, but I'm promoting you to a lead investigator."

Was this Dean's doing? Was this his way of getting me out of the bodyguard business? Or had my eight years of hard work finally paid off? Why wasn't I more excited about the prospect? This was beyond what I'd hoped for. After seeing man after man hired after me move up the ladder, I'd be the first female at Ian's Security to be a lead investigator.

"I'm heading up to Billings' suite. We'll talk more when this is over."

Over? But I didn't want this assignment to be over. Over meant Dean and I were over. Would Dean go back to his models and actresses? Would I go back to being Reeves? My stomach roiled. Maybe I was coming down with Dean's plague. But I was in denial like him. I tossed the bratwurst in the garbage.

I couldn't worry about the future now. I had a job to do.

IF I HAD been sitting, I'd be on the edge of my seat, but instead I was standing on it so I could see over everyone else who was standing as the clock ticked down. Some of the players' wives held hands, and others clasped their hands as if they were praying. The crowd noise was deafening. Down by five, the Kings needed a touchdown, and at the ten-yard line with fifteen seconds left to play, the Kings were poised to take the lead for the win.

I looked away. One part of me couldn't watch, knowing how important a victory was to Dean, while another part of me knew I should be scanning the stadium for threats. Should be. I returned my gaze to the field. He took the snap and the clock ticked down to fourteen, thirteen, twelve, eleven...

And then he threw a bullet to his receiver in the end zone, who at first bobbled the catch, and then drew it to his body for the score.

The fans roared, bouncing up and down like eighty thousand pogo sticks. My happiness for Dean was short-lived as fans started to hop over the fencing. My training kicked in. On autopilot I jumped from the seat and sprinted down the steps to the fence.

A cop grabbed me as I hit the sideline and I flipped my VIP pass. *Wrong girl, buddy.* Hopefully, they were as diligent with everyone else, but with the media and fans swarming the field, control would be impossible.

Blood pounded in my veins and I gulped in air like I raced a marathon. Panic threatened to take over the training. This was when it would happen. I knew it in my bones.

Where the fuck were Oslo and Williams?

A crowd surrounded Dean as Samantha Jameson interviewed the star of the game. I darted over and took stock. From the other side of the mob, I spotted a Stars cheerleader. That was odd. Why would a Stars cheerleader try to congratulate the Kings' quarterback? Then recognition lit my brain. The girl from the bar, dressed like the opponent's cheerleaders. Hell, maybe she was.

"Purple Rain is approaching. Stars cheerleader." Only static crackled from my earpiece.

Damn it to hell! My fingers itched for my gun, but with so many people milling about, it would be reckless to draw. All I could do was throw myself at Dean and hope the crazed cheerleader didn't have a gun and take a head shot. But I had to get to him first. Using my height to my advantage, I snaked my way through the crowd, my heart pounding in fear that I wouldn't get to Dean in time. That I would lose him.

And I'd never told him that I'd fallen in love with him. He'd think I saved him because it was my job, but it was so much more than that. This was personal. This was real. This was love.

As I reached within a foot of Dean, he looked up. Our gazes locked, and I knew I had to tell him, just in case... in case...

I leapt into his arms. "I love you, Dean."

Chapter 14

Dean

I CAUGHT ALEXA as she hit me with the full force of her body, like she was channeling a three-hundred-pound defensive tackle. Alexa loved me? Something was wrong. The cool professional bodyguard wouldn't jump into my arms with declarations of love in front of stadium full of people unless...

Fuck. I looked up just as Alexa shouted in my ear to get down. Like a scene out of a B-movie horror flick, a cheerleader with a crazed look in her eyes and raised a knife, lunged at us. Us? A downward thrust would surely hit Alexa.

Still in the zone from dodging linebackers all day, my reflexes didn't fail me this time. I turned my body and dropped to the ground with Alexa in my arms, landing hard on top of her. She grunted her displeasure. My body covered every inch of her precious yet foolish self.

"Motherfucker," I heard Oslo yell from behind me. "It's clear. I got the bitch."

LIZ MATIS

To be safe, I kept Alexa protected even as she struggled beneath me. I lifted my head to see the screaming crowd disperse as a dozen cops swarmed in to take control of the scene. Jameson, the star reporter who'd been in tougher situations than this, refused to budge, asking her cameraman if he got it all. Despite the chaos in this corner of the field, the celebration was in full swing.

"Get off of me," Alexa yelled. Wiggling, she sputtered, "Oh, God. Now I know what it feels like to be tackled."

She was joking about this? What if the psycho cheerleader had had a gun? What if she'd thrown the knife? Alexa could've been killed. I could have lost her. Fury rose in my blood. How dare she take a chance like that?

Lifting myself off, I grabbed her shoulders and shook, hoping some sense would rattle loose in that stubborn brain of hers. "You little fool. Don't ever do that again."

"It's my job." She struggled to a sitting position.

"To die for me?"

"Yes."

"If you had died, then she might as well have killed me too, Alexa."

She winced and dropped her gaze.

Realizing how tight my hold was, I loosened my grip. "What good would living be without you? I may be just a job to you, but you're more than my bodyguard."

She was shaking on her own with no help for me.

I lifted her chin. Tears streamed down her face. *Aww, fuck.* I hadn't meant to make her cry. "I love you, Alexa. If something happens to you, it happens to me."

"That's just the adrenaline talking."

Maybe it was. I sounded like a babbling love-struck fool. "Is that why you said you loved me?"

"I… I was trying to get your attention." She wiped her tears away and looked nervously around like she was embarrassed.

"Little liar."

"Hey, don't worry about me. Just a scratch," Oslo said. The police handcuffed the stalker.

"I love you, Dean," the cheerleader screamed as she was hauled away. Yeah, she gave a whole new meaning to *love you to death.* I had no idea who she was or why she would want me dead.

Once she was out of sight I stood, offering my hand to Alexa. Ignoring it, she sprang up on her own to attend to Oslo's injury.

"It's just a scratch," she agreed.

"But… but, I'm going to need stitches," pouted Oslo. I laughed at the big and tough bodyguard's expression.

"Butterfly ones," Alexa said as if her coworker had only received a paper cut instead of a deep slice to the skin.

"I would shake your hand, but…" I nodded to the slash that needed more than butterfly stitches. "Thanks, bro."

"Whoa! You thank him and I get yelled at?" Alexa's voice rose.

Samantha stuck a microphone between us. "Walker, why was the Stars cheerleader trying to kill you?"

Both Alexa and I turned our heads. I was going to tell Samantha to fuck off. What Alexa would have said to the reporter remained a mystery as Ryan Terell—the retired tight end for the Cougars and current sports analyst for the network—pulled his wife away. "Jesus, Samantha, trouble follows you everywhere."

"I have a nose for news. And I'm fine. Thanks for asking."

"I can see that. Now leave them alone."

"It's my job," Samantha told her husband.

Where had I heard that before? Alexa crossed her arms and gave me a smug look as Samantha stuck the microphone back in my face.

"Not now," I said.

"Walker promises you an exclusive." Terell looked from his wife to me, nodding his head. "Don't you, Walker?"

"Absolutely." I'd agree to anything to make this all go away for now. I should be celebrating with my teammates. And then there was Alexa, who was not acting like the adoring girlfriend I had hoped she would be now that my stalker had been caught.

Carlos pushed his way through. "What are you doing? They're ready to present the divisional trophy. You're the MVP."

It seemed like more than half the stadium, including my agent, had no idea what had just happened. The police officer in charge said, "Go ahead. You can answer questions later."

Still I hesitated to leave Alexa. I squeezed her shoulders. "Are you okay?"

"Of course I am. Go."

"We'll figured out everything later," I called over my shoulder.

As I accepted the trophy, so many emotions whirled inside me that I had to choke back tears. Elation and pride from this win, sadness that my father wasn't there to share it with me, happiness that I knew my mom was watching it on television, and the remnants of panic and fear of Alexa risking her life for me. I was now determined to win it all, the big game and my only love.

I was one step away from my dream of a Super Bowl Championship, but it wouldn't be the same without Alexa to share it with me. Somehow I had to convince her that I needed her more than Ian's Security did. Convince her that I needed her more than my own life.

Chapter 15

Alexa

I SMILED AT Dean as he came out of the players exit, but his expression was anything but happy.

"I'm driving."

"Okayyyyy." I tossed him the keys and got in on the passenger side, dumbfounded at his attitude. After weeks of me driving him around, I was sure he couldn't wait to get behind the wheel again. That didn't explain the tightness in his jaw or the short, clipped way he'd spoken to me.

Why was he acting like I had offended him—*no*, like I'd hurt him?

Knowing he could easily catch a ride home, I had thoughts of deserting him at the stadium. I was afraid of the awkward conversation once he realized that it was the adrenaline talking. When he realized he didn't love me. I feared we were about to have that conversation.

I'd liked to say that I was brave, but the truth was I'd rather face a physical confrontation than an emotional one. While Dean had been celebrating on the field, answering football questions in the locker room, and then giving the police his official statement, I'd been privy to the initial questioning of the crazy cheerleader, Brandi Dobbs. And something nagged in the back of my mind.

She'd confessed to trying to hurt Dean and even leaving me the flowers as a warning to back off, but she'd denied writing the threatening letters. Of course, this could be a way of avoiding a premeditated murder count making it easier for her to claim insanity.

But if she was telling the truth then Dean was still in danger.

And that's why I didn't run.

I knew I was over-thinking it, worse, making an excuse to stay close to Dean. More than halfway into the ride, I couldn't take the quiet, so I engaged in conversation with something safe. "You had a great game."

Silence.

"Okay, what's up?"

He put on the blinker and made a turn. "We'll talk about it when we get home."

Home. Funny, how I'd come to think of his apartment that way. We'd never spoken about what would happen after my assignment ended. Going back to my little apartment would be lonely, though I'd never thought of myself as being so. I had my work. I had

Joffrey. I had my family. It had always been enough. Until I fell in love with Dean.

But right now he seemed down right mad at me. Why? *Crap.* He must have found out. "Is this about the other letters."

"Damn right it is," he ground out between clenched teeth.

I knew my silence on the matter would come back to bite me. "Our collective bosses decided against informing you."

"And you went right along because you knew I'd have you removed from my detail."

"Exactly. I was your best bet to stay alive."

"Any one of Ian's goons could have done what you did today."

"Oh yeah? Oslo would have been there a second too late. And that's all it takes. And like, you're welcome." I folded my arms across my chest in a huff.

I noticed a smile lifting at the corner of his mouth. Dean parked the car, cut the engine, and turned toward me.

"Can't you do something else?"

"Like what?"

"Like… like run the anti-bullying program you want me to start. You would do more good there than as a bodyguard."

"But—"

"You know that I'm right. Now who's being stubborn?"

"What I am is not qualified. I'm not accepting a job simply because I'm Dean Walker's girlfriend."

"You weren't qualified to be a bodyguard once."

He wasn't going to let this go, but just because I loved him didn't mean I was going to let him control my life. And I wasn't about to tell him about the promotion Ian had offered me. "You can't tell me what to do."

"Obviously. But that doesn't mean we're not going to fight about it." Dean got out of the car and slammed the door.

Stunned, I didn't move. What did that mean? Dean opened my door and offered me his hand. Now I was really confused. I slid out of the seat and up against his body.

He cupped my chin, leaned down, and breathed a thank you over my lips. Then he kissed me gently. "Alexa, don't be mad at me for wanting to keep you safe."

He took my hand as we walked from the garage to his building. I tried to clear my head, reminding myself of my nagging suspicion that danger still stalked Dean. With the threat eliminated, Ian's men were no longer watching the apartment.

Out of habit, I checked all the rooms before joining Dean in the kitchen.

"Need a beer?" Dean asked.

"Hell yeah," I said as he handed me one.

Dean opted for a meal that was heating up in the microwave.

"Guess you're feeling better?"

"Yeah, the IV really helped. But this is just soup. Mrs. McKenna made it specially for me." He pointed to a Get Well Soon card on the counter.

"McKenna? As in your backup quarterback?"

"Yeah, his mom owns Paleo Planet."

"The place that makes all your meals? And also delivers to the Kings' front office?" I picked up the card.

"Um, yeah. Why?" The buzzer of the microwave dinged.

My blood chilled as I read Mrs. McKenna's words.

Congrats on the big win. I made a very, very special meal just for you.

The words *very, very* confirmed my suspicions. What an idiot I was! Dean brought the spoon to his lips and blew. Before he could take a sip, I smacked the spoon down and away. Liquid splattered on the cabinet and the floor.

"Alexa! What the fuck?"

All the times Dean complained about his stomach and I never thought of foul play. Poison. Arsenic, if I had to guess. Perhaps I wasn't qualified to be a lead investigator either. How could I have missed it?

"Look." I held up the inside of the card. "Does something look familiar?"

Dean studied it. Then read it out loud. "Congrats on the big win. I made a…" His eyes went wide with shock as realization dawned on him. Dean went to chuck the container in the sink.

"No! It has to be sent for testing. And you'll want a complete blood workup."

Dean shook his head in disbelief as he placed the food on the counter. "Why would she try to poison me?"

I started to pace the galley kitchen. "So her son wouldn't be the backup anymore." I turned to Dean. "Do you think he could be involved?"

"I don't know what to think."

Dean looked like a man in shock, but I continued in a matter-of-fact tone. "She must have planted the letters so the police would concentrate on a jilted lover if the autopsy revealed the poison."

"Autopsy? Fuck. Alexa?"

I stopped pacing and looked up.

"You saved me a second time today."

"It's my job."

"Fuck your job."

"I'd rather fuck you."

A smiled lifted at the corner of his mouth. "You want to fuck me, but you don't love me?"

"I do love you. Why, I don't know. Two women in

the span of three hours tried to kill you."

"Then it's settled."

"What?"

"I need to be watched twenty-four seven. And I can't think of anything more effective than a wife keeping tabs on me."

If there wasn't mischief in his wide smile, I would've kicked him the way I taught Tammy—and not in the shins. "A wife? If that's a proposal, then it's a piss-poor one."

"Give me a break. I almost got killed today. Twice."

"My answer is a negative." Even if he'd been on bended knee or both knees, begging me, I wasn't ready to say yes. "I love you, Dean, but we both need time to decompress from this. To know for certain that what we have is real."

My heart knew the truth of my love for Dean, but I wasn't so certain of his feelings. Not that I thought he was lying, but from the way we met and the way I was forced upon him and his life, I needed to know that Dean's heart belonged to me. And that his proposal wasn't the result of some misplaced sense of gratitude for saving his life.

"I'll take that as a maybe." He lips descended on mine. Urgent. Passionate. Making me want to change my answer from a no to a yes.

"What now?" he asked.

"I'll call Ian and let him take care of the details with the police."

"Great. While you do that, I'll order us a pizza."

My finger hovered over Ian's number. "Yeah, I told you that health-food shit would kill you."

"See what I mean? I need a wife."

"And what do I get out of the deal?"

"Since you don't want a man to protect that hot body of yours, then I'll be the man to safeguard your heart."

Yet today he'd proved he would protect me from physical harm, shielding my body with his. We'd saved each other.

Epilogue

Alexa

THE KINGS HAD done a spectacular job of decorating the training facility for the Super Bowl ring ceremony. In the darkened cavern of the open space, spotlights shone from the ceiling of the dome. A movie screen played a continuous loop of season highlights. A huge dance floor in the center was ready for dancing after dinner. Tables decorated in the team colors of blue and gold lined all four sides of the room. The lit up centerpieces looked like a miniature version of the Times Square Ball on New Year's Eve. Tonight was a sporting event all unto its own.

In the four months since the Super Bowl win, I had officially moved in with Dean. After one last gig guarding a set of twin toddlers as a nanny, I'd accepted Ian's offer as a lead investigator. With the better hours, I'd be able to spend more time with Dean, including working alongside him on his anti-bullying program.

Dean looked devilish in his made-to-order black suit

and gold tie. As yummy as he looked clothed, I couldn't wait to get home and use that tie as a blindfold. Or to bind his wrists. The slinky gold wrap dress Joffrey selected for me was designed to come off with just a pull at the side-bow. Dean had already tugged at twice before we left our apartment. *Ours.*

Dean had given me free rein to redecorate, not that I was much of an interior designer, but now it was a home instead of a bachelor pad.

An announcement was made to go to our seats. Some of Dean's offensive line shared our table along with their wives. A black box sat in front of each of the players' plates, but there was also one with my name etched in gold. "What's this?"

Dean ran a hand lovingly along the box in front of him. "Support staff get rings too. You worked for Billings. It's not the same one as the players get. Less obscenely gaudy, from what I understand."

"But I didn't help the team win."

He looked at me. "Of course you helped. How far do you think they would've gotten without me?"

Before I could say anything in response, Dean kissed me. With one touch of lips, he could not only shut me up but make me forget what I was about to say.

From the podium, Billings said, "Are you ready to see your Super Bowl Championship ring?" A resounding cheer went up from the crowd. "On three. One, two, three. Do it!"

This was Dean's moment, and I wanted to share it with him. His eyes lit up as he opened the case. He slid the ring on his finger, fisted his hand and kissed his prize. It *was* obscenely gaudy. A jeweled emblem of a raised gold crown sat in the center of the diamond-encrusted ring. Tiny white diamond footballs topped the five points of the crown.

"Wow! That is spectacular," I said.

Dean nodded and gestured to the box I had pushed aside. "Aren't you going to open yours?"

I flipped open the case. I either had the wrong box or someone was playing a joke on me. Set off against the deep blue velvet cushion, a ring with a canary-yellow heart-shaped diamond the size of my knuckle stared back at me. The color reminded me of the flecks of gold in Dean's eyes. A halo of tiny white diamonds surrounded the center stone. It had to be a beautiful mistake.

"This is not a Super Bowl ring," I said, looking up at Dean, who instead of admiring his ring was smiling and looking at me expectantly.

"I switched it out. I have it in my pocket." Dean fell to a bended knee. "Hopefully this is better than my last 'piss-poor proposal,' as you called it. Will you marry me, Alexa? Let me forever watch over you the way you've watched over me."

He slipped the engagement ring on my finger, but I

only had eyes for him, reveling in the way he looked at me. With hope. With love. So much that it overwhelmed me and I felt tears well in my eyes.

"Yes, I'll marry you."

A cheer sounded as we kissed. My heart did a little cheer of its own as Dean's mouth claimed mine.

The rest of the night Dean and his teammates showed off their championship rings, mugging for the cameras while I flashed my engagement ring and my scaled-down version of the Kings' bling. One ring for each hand. One for each side of me. The bodyguard and the quarterback's fiancée.

Guarding the Quarterback

The End

Dear Reader,

Thank you for taking the time to read Guarding the Quarterback. If you enjoyed it, please consider telling your friends or posting a short review. Word of mouth is an author's best friend and much appreciated.

Please signup for my newsletter at www.lizmatis.com

Love sports romances? Check out Romancing the Jock Group on Facebook!
facebook.com/groups/RomancingtheJock

About the Author

Liz Matis is a mild mannered accountant by day and romance author by night. Married 30 years she believes in happily-ever-after!

Fun Fact: Liz read her first romance at the age of fifteen and soon after wrote her first romances starring her friends and their latest crushes!

Fun Fact 2: Liz keeps an inspiration board for all her books on Pinterest. Check it out here:
pinterest.com/lizmatis

Keep in touch with Liz at:

Website:

www.lizmatis.com

Blog:

www.taoofliz.blogspot.com

Email:

elizabethmatis@gmail.com

Twitter:

@LizMatis

Facebook:

Liz Matis Fan Page

Goodreads:

goodreads.com/author/show/5289185.Liz_Matis

To sign up for my newsletter please see signup on via my website:

www.lizmatis.com

Coming Soon

Playing for Gelato –
Champions of the Heart – Book 2

Also by Liz Matis

Fantasy Football Romance Series Box Set

From bestselling author, Liz Matis, comes the box set of the popular Fantasy Football Romance series! Includes the award-winning and #1 bestseller in Sports Fiction, Playing For Keeps, along with Going For It – also a #1 bestseller in Sports Fiction, Huddle Up, and The Quarterback Sneak, which also reached #1. The series has over 600 four and five stars reviews on Goodreads!

Or start the series with Playing For Keeps

Journalist Samantha Jameson always wanted to be one of the boys, but Ryan Terell won't let her join the club. Fresh from the battlegrounds of Iraq, reporting on a bunch of overgrown boys playing pro football is just the change of scenery she needs. If trying to be taken seriously in the world of sports writing wasn't hard enough, Ryan, her college crush, is only making it harder. As a tight-end for the team she's covering, he is strictly off limits.

Ryan Terell is a playmaker on and off the field, but when Samantha uncovers his moves, he throws out the playbook. Just as he claims his sweetest victory, Samantha's investigation into a steroid scandal involving his team forces him to call a time-out to their off the record trysts. But then a life threatening injury on the field will force them both to decide just how far they'll go to win the game.

Winner of the NECRWA First Kiss Contest.

Other books by Liz...

Summer Dreaming by Liz Matis

I'm looking for a hero. Not.

You'd think as a new college grad I'd be looking for the perfect job and the perfect man. Well, I'm not. Summer is here and instead of plotting my future, I'm playing in the Hamptons with my two best friends. Sun and sex is all I'm looking for. Then I meet Sean Dempsey, my fantasy lifeguard in the flesh. But he is more than just a hot bod with a whistle. And after he makes a daring save, I'm thinking a hero is exactly what I've been looking for all along.

To the rescue...

By day I guard the beaches in the Hamptons, by

night I've had my fair share of summer flings. Then I meet Kelsey Mitchell, a girl with eyes like the setting sun and I burn for more. Something I have no right to ask of her…forever.

Love burns hotter in the Hamptons. Come play.

Love By Design by Liz Matis

Design Intervention starts the second season with its own surprise makeover. Interior designer Victoria Bryce must break in her temporary co-host, Aussie Russ Rowland.

Sparks fly on camera as they argue over paint colors and measurement mishaps leading to passions igniting behind the scenes. But when their pasts collide with the present will the foundation they built withstand the final reveal? An HGTV meets Sex and the City romp!

Real Men Don't Drink Appletinis by Liz Matis

Hollywood's handsomest men surround celebrity agent Ava Gardner but none are as intriguing as larger-than-life Grady O'Flynn. The Navy SEAL is on an unsanctioned mission when they end up starring in their own romantic comedy.

Will they continue to sizzle when Grady has to report back to duty? In this sexy novelette by Liz Matis, two lovers have two weeks to find out.